IF

FOREVER

Comes

A.L. JACKSON

A.L. Jackson
www.aljacksonauthor.com
Cover Design by RBA Designs
Photo by **Perrywinkle Photography.**
Formatting by Mesquite Business Services

Print ISBN: 978-1-946420-18-3
eBook ISBN: 978-1-983404-71-9

IF
FOREVER

Comes

More From A.L. Jackson

Confessions of the Heart – NEW SERIES
COMING SOON
More of You
All of Me
Pieces of Us

Fight for Me
Show Me the Way
Hunt Me Down
Lead Me Home – Spring 2018

Bleeding Stars
A Stone in the Sea
Drowning to Breathe
Where Lightning Strikes
Wait
Stay
Stand

The Regret Series
Lost to You
Take This Regret
If Forever Comes

One

I once made a promise that no matter what life brought our way, I would never walk away.

I'd meant it. Every fucking word of it.

But life had taken Elizabeth and me down a path neither of us knew how to navigate. One neither of us could bear. Life sometimes puts so much weight on our shoulders we crumble, bends us so far we break.

It'd broken Elizabeth. Cruelly. Savagely.

In turn, she'd shattered me.

I lifted the glass to my lips. The golden liquid

burned a path down my throat and settled as a pathetic excuse for comfort in the pit of my stomach.

Lifting the glass again, I bled it dry. Ice clanked around in the bottom when I slammed it to the bar. I raked my hand through my hair and palmed the tense muscles in my neck.

Kurt inclined his head toward my glass. "You need another?"

I shrugged and pushed the empty toward him. "Guess so."

He laughed with a mild shake of his head and began to pour me a fresh drink. "You playing coy tonight? I've watched you stumble your sorry ass out of here at closing damn near every night for the last three months. Planning on cutting yourself off early or something?" Sarcasm rolled from the question, and he cocked a disparaging brow.

An incredulous snort shot from my nose. He had me pegged. The only plan I had was drinking myself into a stupor and praying when I woke in the morning, I'd wake from this fucking nightmare and be in Elizabeth's bed.

"Just keep them coming."

He set the tumbler in front of me. "That's what I figured."

The little bar was quiet tonight. I only had to walk two short blocks inland from my condo to seek its seclusion. I'd passed it what seemed a million times when I'd travel to and from Elizabeth's house, and now it'd become some kind of fucked-up refuge that fed the destruction, something to knock me down a little further. Yeah, I knew exactly how to get here, but that didn't mean I wasn't lost.

That's what we were. Both of us. Completely, unbearably lost.

Slumping forward, I propped myself up on my elbow, head supported by my hand. I took a deep swill of my drink, wishing that missing her didn't hurt so bad. It was excruciating.

But I knew in my burning gut that she was hurting worse than I was, more than I could imagine, and that was what was absolutely killing me.

I jumped when a stool skidded against the floor beside me. I cut my eye to whoever thought it necessary to take a seat right beside me in a bar that was nearly deserted.

Matthew.

Of course.

He plopped down onto the stool with a heavy sigh and leaned forward on his elbows.

Kurt approached. "What can I get you, man?"

"Bud Light."

The two of us said nothing while Kurt twisted the cap and slid the beer toward him.

"Thanks," Matthew mumbled.

"Sure thing."

Matthew drew the beer to his mouth, looked ahead without a word as he swallowed hard.

Tension flared between us, this dense weight that thickened the air. On edge, I sipped at my drink and tapped my fingers on the bar, my defenses all wound up and on alert.

"You're a hard man to find," he finally said.

"That's because I don't want to be found."

So obviously that was a lie. All I wanted was for Elizabeth to somehow find her way back to me. What I didn't want was to sit here and listen to Matthew feed me bullshit about how everything was going to be all right. To give it time.

It was always more fucking time. But time only turned around and heaped more sorrow on top of us. And Matthew hadn't suffered through what we had. He hadn't watched the light dim in Elizabeth's eyes. Not the way I had. I wasn't sure any amount of time could rekindle it.

"So is this what you do with yourself night after night when you don't have Lizzie?"

I lifted a noncommittal shoulder. "What? You think I should sit alone in my condo instead?" I released a resentful snort. "Fuck that."

Anger pinged around in my chest. My condo had finally gone under contract too, while Elizabeth and I had searched for the perfect home to raise our family in. But I had to back out of the sale at the last minute so I'd at least have someplace to sleep while the rest of my world fell apart.

Matthew pinned me with a look of disbelief. "So this is better? This is your solution?" His words hardened as he waved an exasperated hand around the room. "Do you think I don't get it, Christian? Do you think I don't know how hard this is for you?"

I shook my head and turned away, tipped my glass back to my mouth. No, I didn't think he *got* it. How the hell could he? He got to crawl in bed with the woman he loved every night, not lie across town from her, wide awake, worrying that might be the exact moment she was breaking into pieces every god-damned minute of the night.

He dipped his head and turned his face up to capture mine. "Do something," he pleaded.

Pain fisted my heart, because I really wanted to, but then the bitterness came surging back. "Like what?" My face pinched. "I fucking tried. I tried and I only made things worse. She won't even look at me when I see her."

"Because she's hurting, Christian."

"Don't you think I realize that? But I can't take that pain away. If I could, I would, but there is absolutely nothing in this world I can do to change what happened."

"So...what? Give up? Pretend that both of you

aren't miserable without each other?" Frustrated, Matthew forced his stool back from the bar and stood, dug out his wallet and tossed a ten on the counter. He turned to leave, hesitating, then took an aggressive step toward me.

"You know what, Christian? I had faith in you. You promised you'd never walk away from her again, and I believed you. You promised to be there through thick and thin..." He vibrated, seemed to try to calm himself as he ran a hand over his crop of brown hair. "Well, this is the thin, and it fucking sucks. I know that. And I know you're hurting every bit as much as she is. But *this,* right now"—he jabbed his finger on the bar—"is when that promise counts. Not when everything is going like you planned."

My attention dropped to my fingers where I had a stranglehold on the half-empty glass. Harsh words dripped from my mouth. "She doesn't *want* me, Matthew. She made it clear she'd rather die than let me touch her again. Believe me, if there was any chance I could win her back, I'd take it. But there's not. Elizabeth already made her decision."

"You fought so hard for her. Now look at you." He shook his head in disgust. "You're a damned fool."

He left me sitting there in my misery.

I drained the last of my drink. Slumping over on

the bar, I buried my face in the crook of my elbow.

My head hurt. My heart hurt.

Everything just fucking hurt.

My eyes fluttered as my thoughts swam, and I got lost somewhere between fantasy and reality.

two

I clicked the door shut behind us and flicked the lock. Elizabeth backed into the middle of the room, those warm brown eyes never looking away from me. I rushed her, hungrily palming her hips as my mouth descended on the sweetness of hers. "I've been dying to get you alone all night," I grumbled as I jerked her against my body.

Elizabeth giggled, all throaty and warm. The deep burr vibrated against my lips. It reminded me so much of all those times I had her pinned against my apartment wall, back when we'd wandered these same New York City streets when we were in college. This woman I held in my arms felt so much like the eighteen-year-old I'd held all those years before, back when our bodies had explored, back when she'd grown from the innocent girl I'd first met into this sexy woman who very nearly lived in my bed. Back then she'd flirted and teased, had set me on fire, left me begging for more.

And damn if it didn't feel amazing to have her back.

"Now that you have me alone, just what is it you intend to do with me?" she teased, tugging at my tie.

We'd been out to dinner to celebrate the new life we were beginning. Lizzie had gotten all dressed up in the most adorable dress, her black hair tied up in ribbons. And Elizabeth... God, one look and she stole my breath. The city was in the grip of winter, and she was wearing a belted sweater dress that cinched around her narrow waist, flowing down to perfectly hug the curve of her hips. It came to rest just above her knees. There, just a strip of bare skin teased me before it gave way to black high-heeled boots. My attention shot to the diamond ring that danced on her finger. I still couldn't believe she'd let me put it there. God, I couldn't wait to marry her.

"What *don't* I intend to do with you would be the better question," I murmured, wrapping my palm around the back of her neck, the other possessive at her waist. I kissed her hard, devoured the shocked breath of air that slipped up her throat, stroked my tongue across hers. I kissed her and kissed her and kissed her because I was never going to stop.

Our suite bedroom had floor-to-ceiling windows that faced the street far below us. Outside, the city glowed. Winter bore down, and snowflakes fluttered toward the ground as they were set free from the inky sky. Lights glimmered through the haze, spilling a soft glow into our darkened room.

I pushed her up against the window. Elizabeth grunted. She sagged against the expansive sheet of glass, the perfect lines of her body silhouetted against the backdrop of the city that seemed to echo my past, the memories so thick, they seemed almost alive.

I took a step back and let my eyes wander over the one who inhabited them all.

Gradually the lines of that beautiful face came into focus, and for a moment, my gaze got lost in the amber warmth of her soft brown eyes. Devotion pumped steadily through my veins. I loved her. Loved her with everything, with my life, with my soul.

And I was going to spend my entire life proving it to her.

My actions were slow and deliberate as I knelt

down in front of her, watching the way her lips parted when I did. I slipped my hands under the hem of her dress, ran them up the softness of her thighs and around to cup her perfect, round bottom, my fingers brushing lace and satin. Her dress was all bunched up on my forearms as I hiked it around her hips. The long length of her toned legs were exposed as she stood there trembling in her boots.

"You have the sweetest ass, Elizabeth," I whispered as I burrowed my fingers into the delicate flesh. There was no stopping the overwhelming rush of need that burned through my system when I touched her this way. Flames licked at my skin and pulsed heat into my veins.

Every single inch of my body hardened.

"You always have," I said as I stared up at her. "Do you know that? The first time I saw you ten years ago in that little cafe, all I could think about was finding out what you had hidden underneath your clothes. And it's perfection, Elizabeth. Every inch of you is perfection."

Elizabeth watched down on me with dark, hungry eyes. Deliberately my hand slid around to her front. My tongue darted out to wet my lips as I nudged her legs farther apart. I ran my knuckles over the scrap of dampened lace between her thighs.

Vibrations shook her, and she grasped my

shoulders for support. "Christian," pushed from her lungs in a quiet plea, her fingers desperate as they curled in my shirt.

My name on her tongue sounded like heaven.

I suppressed a pained groan and let my hands trail back down her legs to the top of her boots. I sat back a little, one knee on the floor and the other bent with my foot planted in front of me. I brought her foot up to rest on my knee. "I want you to remember this night, Elizabeth." Slowly I dragged the zipper down the inside of her leg to her ankle. The distinct sound infiltrating the hush of the room slammed me with a shot of lust, curled as the tightest knot in the pit of my stomach. I had to will myself to keep it under control, to go slow, because I wanted to savor this night. "I want you to forever remember the first time I make love to you in the city where we started all those years ago."

I wanted this night to erase every bad memory she harbored of this place while it took her back to the hundreds of perfect nights we'd spent with our bodies tangled.

I wanted this to make a mark. An impression.

I wanted it to make a promise.

I worked her boot free, watching her expression as it dropped to the floor with a soft thunk.

Elizabeth emitted a tiny whimper, quivered more.

Quietly I went to work on the other.

Anticipation thickened the air around us, ours breaths filling the room, heavy and hard. Both of our bodies strained, knowing the pleasure that was to come. Elizabeth and I had wasted so much time. *Too* much time. How many nights had been pilfered away when we could have been wrapped up in each other like we were going to be tonight? No more. I was finished squandering away my chances, finished living my life as a fool.

My life would be lived for her.

And I'd never get enough.

I edged back to take her in.

Barefooted, she squirmed in front of me, her palms flattened against the window to hold herself up. Her expression was dark, intense, needy…as needy as my own. Soft fingertips came out to brush along my cheek, set me aflame as they glanced across my lips.

"You are such a beautiful man," she murmured as a somber flash of emotion flitted over her face. "Inside and out. Thank you for showing me. For making me finally see. For helping me believe. I'd forgotten how to."

With her adoring touch, a shiver rolled down my spine, spun with my desire, wound with the devotion that filled every crevice of my being. She was mine. But God, there was no doubt that I belonged to her.

"I won't ever let you forget again." The promise penetrated the heady air.

Steadily I pushed to my feet, my gaze locked on hers, my intentions clear. I unbuckled her belt, let it fall free before I fisted her dress and dragged it over her head. Waves of her hair fell all around her delicate shoulders, her nearly naked body like a beacon that called me home. I took her by the hips and hoisted her up. She wrapped her long legs around my waist, just as sure as the arms she wrapped around my neck. Her tiny body burned into mine as she pressed herself to me.

My spirit sang.

With one arm secured around her waist, I twisted the other hand through the thick locks of blonde that shimmered in the faint glow of light cast in from the window.

Elizabeth brushed her lips across mine, then sucked at my bottom lip before she turned her attention to the top. A greedy urge to consume her speared me when she swept her tongue over mine in a slow, measured tease.

A growl rumbled in my chest, and I felt her smiling against my mouth, all cute and smug.

My hold intensified as I carried her toward the huge bed that rested in the middle of the room.

This girl was too much. One touch and she managed to devour me whole.

But tonight, I would be the one doing the

devouring.

I dropped her onto the bed. She bounced on the plush mattress, and that hoarse giggle from earlier made a resurgence. A coy smile curved her perfect mouth as she stared up at me.

"And just what do you think you're laughing about?" I warned, fighting the humor that threatened to work its way into my tone. I stepped back and tugged at the knot in my tie. I pulled it free, dropped it to the ground. I ticked through the buttons on my shirt, one by one, while I matched her penetrating gaze.

Sitting up on her elbows, she rubbed her thighs together, watching as I peeled my shirt from my shoulders. Her voice was all raspy. "I'm laughing because I can't stop, Christian. I can't express what being with you means to me. I never thought I'd feel this way again. How can I even begin to describe how *good* I feel?"

I edged forward and placed my hands on her knees. "Prepare yourself to feel like this night after night, day after day, Elizabeth. I'm not ever going to stop loving you." I forced her legs apart. My attention went straight to her lace-covered center. I dipped down and pressed my mouth to the thin fabric, softly kissed her there. "Not ever going to stop touching you."

Elizabeth jerked. The muscles of her flat belly rippled with the slow tremor that rolled through her body as I flattened my tongue on the lace in a long, firm stroke. She writhed. "Oh my God, Christian," begged from her mouth.

Her smell, the sounds escaping her quivering mouth, the need I felt radiating from her worked my body into a slow frenzy.

I slipped off the bed, grabbed her by the thighs, and tugged her to the very edge of the mattress. I wrapped my fingers in her panties, and she lifted her legs in the most delicious way, one foot pressed to my chest, the other to the top of my thigh.

Fuck.

There were few words to describe her. I couldn't help but tell her the only one that sufficed. "Perfect. You are absolutely perfect, Elizabeth. No one compares to you. No one."

It was her. Only her.

The only one there'd ever been.

I edged back and pulled her panties down the length of her legs, tossing them aside.

Faster than I could make sense of it, Elizabeth scrambled to her knees, the woman kneeling in front of me wearing only the sexiest bra I'd ever seen in my life, all black and lace and frill. The rest of that luscious body was exposed, her skin smooth and kissed in honey, just begging for my touch.

I ached, couldn't wait to bury myself in the heat

hidden between her thighs.

She raked her fingers down my chest. My stomach twisted in knots as she dragged them through the trail of hair that disappeared into my pants. Her expression was intense, filled with all-consuming need and overpowering love as she forcefully jerked the button free on my slacks, her breath all sweet as it fanned out around me.

It felt like the most sublime contradiction.

She leaned in close, never looking away from my face as she lowered the zipper on my pants, just as slowly as I'd lowered the ones on her boots. The waistband hung loose.

The words bled from her mouth where it rested just a breath from mine, washed over me in an intoxicating swell. "Ten years, Christian, and it's still the same. You consume me." Her fingers teased at the waistband of my underwear. "You still manage to make my stomach feel like it's bottoming out and my heart beat like it might pound right out of my chest." There was no mistaking the passion wound tightly through the words. "You make me *ache*." The last came with the same desperation thundering through my veins.

Her movements were dense, as dense as the air, weighted with fervency. She swallowed. "It's always been you, Christian. Since the moment I realized I was in love with you when I was eighteen, I never stopped. And I promise you, I'm not ever going to."

Lust curled through me as she ran her hands beneath the fabric of my pants and pushed them down over my hips. They sat open at my thighs. My erection strained for her as she knelt in front of me. Through my briefs, she delicately ran her thumb around the ridge of sensitive skin. My stomach quivered and jerked.

"Elizabeth," rumbled from my mouth, "that feels so good."

Her touch became firmer, purposed as she palmed me through the fabric in a calculated taunt. Then she freed me. With one hand she grasped me behind my neck and leaned her weight back, her hair falling and brushing along the bed as her body arched. With her other hand, she pleasured me with long, hard strokes that nearly brought me to my knees. "Fuck." The word came harsh, grated from my throat.

A satisfied grin lifted her mouth, quivered at just one side. "This…this is the way you make me feel, like I'm going to come undone with just the barest caress. Or maybe I'll come with just the way you're looking at me right now."

I groaned, consumed—floored—loving this girl more than I ever thought possible. Sexy and sweet. Innocent and unbelievably bold. She was everything.

Everything.

I rushed to get undressed, kicking off my shoes and socks in the same second I shook my pants free from my legs. Elizabeth was pushing my underwear down just as frantically as I was twisting out of them. I forced her back onto the bed.

She lay there panting, completely exposed.

My groan echoed off the walls when I sank deep into her warmth.

A thrill rocketed straight up my spine, spun my head with a delirious joy. I fisted my hands in her hair, my hips rigid as I rocked into her.

Elizabeth clenched around me, her body fitting me like she was made for me.

Because she was.

"Oh, fuck, Elizabeth." I pulled back and slammed back into her.

She gasped, lifting her chin with her mouth open wide.

"Nothing could feel better than this," raked from my throat. "Nothing in this world. Nothing."

Pleasure fisted me, pulled at the knots that already twisted my stomach in the tightest ball. I kissed her hard, just as hard as I drove my body into hers, determined to lose myself deeper in her than I ever had before.

Elizabeth's hands were everywhere, impatient, greedy as they sought me out, sinking into my shoulders, digging into my ass. She lifted herself to me in a desperate play to bring me closer, offering up every inch of that glorious body.

I took her whole, fierce, hard, frantic. She was fire and warmth and light. My joy. My life.

My fingers dug into her hips, and I rose up onto my knees. She wrapped her legs around my waist, and I lifted her as I buried myself in her again and again.

Elizabeth was panting, these short, rasping sounds forced from her mouth. Her body rocked with each firm thrust. Her breasts swelled over the cup of her bra, her hair spread out all around her as she gripped the sheets.

"Beautiful," I wheezed. "I wish you could see what you look like right now. What I see when I look at you."

Her gaze met mine, full of meaning that spoke of our hearts, of our pasts, of our futures. "I already see it in your eyes."

Her legs began to shake.

Forever.

I drove into her.

And I could feel it when she came, could feel her pleasure as she clenched around my cock. That pleasure rose in waves, lifting her back from the bed as she cried out my name.

I slammed into her, devouring her, taking what had always been mine.

Hooking her legs over my arms, I gripped her by the back of the waist, would do anything to get her closer. Leaning back, I lifted my face toward the ceiling and let myself go.

Forever.

Ecstasy hit me. Intensely. Wholly. I throbbed as I poured into her, this bliss that spread out to saturate every cell of my body.

Forever.

Elizabeth was my forever.

I twitched and jerked. Inhaling raggedly, I sucked air into my empty lungs. I attempted to loosen my fingers anchored in her flesh.

Elizabeth gasped for a breath of her own. I slumped down on top of her, feeling an absurd grin spread across my face as I did. But I couldn't stop it. I was happy. So happy, it contented every cell within me, erased every dark night I'd ever spent without her.

I kissed her on the mouth and leaned up on my elbow to brush back the sweat-dampened hair matted to her forehead.

She smiled, her eyes all alight with the love that would never let us go.

My pulse stuttered.

Elizabeth would never stop stealing my breath.

Because she possessed my soul.

Her brown eyes blinked up at me, and a soft, sleepy smile spread across her full lips.

"What are we waiting for, Elizabeth?" came as an unstoppable request from the depths of my soul. I pulled back. One hand gripped her hip as I searched her face.

Softly her lips parted, her presence invading my space, stealing my senses.

"What do you mean?" she asked. Her expression worked to grasp my meaning, a hunch clearly taking hold in the line that dented her brow.

"Waiting to get married…waiting to add to our family. What are we waiting for? This is what we both want. It's what's good for us. What's good for Lizzie. I know we planned on waiting, but…"

After everything we'd been through in the last year, me making contact with my daughter for the first time in her life, just days before she turned five, the way Elizabeth and I had struggled through the months as she'd tried to shut me out, the disaster we'd created in the wake of this passion that could never be contained. And our reconciliation that had finally cut through all the shit that had held us back. We'd thought it best to wait. To give ourselves time to adjust to this new life, to learn how to be the family we were always meant to be.

But that's what we already were.

A family.

I wanted it in name. I wanted it in reality.

The words rushed up my throat, flooded from my mouth. "I want it all, and I want it now. I want it with you, Elizabeth."

"Christian—"

"Please, don't say anything right now. I just want you to think about it."

She grabbed my face. "I don't need to think about it. I'm ready for this. I'm ready for you. I'm ready for *us*. There are no questions left."

Then she smiled, a twist of her mouth that said it all.

Relief and joy escaped me in a throaty groan. It was all I wanted, to spend my life with her, to spend it with our daughter, to live for my family, to watch it grow.

Loving fingers trailed down my back, before she wrapped both arms around me in a tender embrace.

Rolling onto my back, I grabbed for her and tugged her flat onto my chest. Everything thrummed between us, the spastic beat of our hearts, our love, the trust that had once again bonded us together.

And I silently swore I'd never do anything to break it again.

I gentled my fingers through her hair, and her breath left her in a contented sigh. We laid like that for what seemed like hours, both of us silent as we stared out the window at the blanket of winter that held in the city lights. Snow still flitted across the sky, and the deepest calm settled over us.

Elizabeth's fingers played at my collarbone, and

she ran lazy circles over my skin as her heart began to slow and find rest with mine. "I'm so happy, Christian." Her voice bled into the dimness of the room like a declaration, a profession made.

Her confession took root somewhere deep inside me and swelled within my chest. I cupped her face and tilted it up so I could look at her, my tone tightened in emphasis.

"You make me happy. You always have. There's something about you, Elizabeth, just being in a room with you, that brings me joy."

She trembled an impassioned smile and ran her fingertips along my bottom lip. "I get to spend my life with my best friend." That smile strengthened with emotion. "There's nothing more perfect than that."

My eyes dropped closed. *My best friend.* They fluttered open to meet with hers. "Perfect."

Everything was perfect.

PRESENT DAY

God, I missed her. Missed her so much it paralyzed me, left me without a will. Because this wasn't about betrayal, not something she or I had caused. This was something that neither of us could control. This was unfair, unjust. This was torture.

"Hey, man, we're getting ready to close up."

Jarred from my stupor, I scrubbed a palm over my face to wake myself up, swayed a little as I tried to find my footing. I struggled to focus as I signed the tab he slid my way.

"You okay?" Kurt asked, eyeing me as he gathered the receipt.

The laugh that escaped me was humorless. "Yeah, I'm fucking *perfect*."

three

Remnants of our devastation simmered just beneath the surface of my skin. A constant, nagging reminder of what I had lost. I'd do anything to purge them from my mind. Yet, at the same time, I clung to them. I clung to the memories that haunted my heart because they somehow comforted me. Those months that I'd been favored enough to spend in Elizabeth's arms, with Lizzie by my side, those days we'd laughed and loved as we'd lost ourselves in expectation—I wanted to hang onto them.

God, I wanted to hang onto Elizabeth.

I rammed the heels of my hands in my eyes.

Fuck.

This wasn't the life we were supposed to be living. I just didn't know how to get through to her, how to break through the pain. How could I make her see?

The residual of last night pounded my head, spun with the overwhelming urge that burned inside to *make this right.* I thought I finally had.

I was so wrong.

The traffic light turned green, and I accelerated as I traveled the seven-point-three miles to Elizabeth's house.

Bitter laughter bounced around the cab of my car.

Seven-point-three miles.

When I came to San Diego more than a year ago and found out just how close Elizabeth and Lizzie lived to me, the short distance had seemed like an affirmation that everything was as it should be. Like maybe things had shifted as they slowly aligned. Like if I just reached out, I'd be close enough to hold Lizzie and Elizabeth in the safety of my arms. That I'd be able to protect them. Love them.

Maybe I was a fool to think that after everything I'd done, I could somehow deserve what Elizabeth had promised.

Because now I knew better.

Seven-point-three miles was a greater distance than I could ever fathom.

God.

Remorse shook me as I glanced in the mirror and changed lanes. We'd come so close to making it. Only one day and Elizabeth would have been my wife. Then one brutal lash of fate had cut us deep. Shattered us in a way that neither of us could have anticipated. That wound had festered. Rotted and decayed. Built and burned until it'd erupted. Elizabeth had cut me from her life just as harshly as the trauma had struck her down.

But it wasn't as if I weren't broken, too.

I crossed those impenetrable miles. Steadily my heart began to pound harder and faster with each second that passed by. Not with the stirring of hope as it'd done all those months when I'd first returned, when I'd done everything I could to make amends for the greatest mistake I'd ever made. Definitely not like it'd done with the overpowering thrill of excitement I'd had when I traveled here after the modest house had become my home.

Now it thudded with the deepest resonance of pain.

On a heavy sigh, I made a left into the quiet neighborhood. I pulled into Elizabeth's driveway, killed the engine, and forced myself to climb out. A cloak of early morning fog sat like an oppressive weight in the gray sky, blanketing me in a heaviness I couldn't escape, even if the sun were to somehow manage to shine. In disinclination, I stuffed my hands in my pants pockets and plodded up her sidewalk to the front door. Drawing in a deep breath, I rapt twice on the door, then turned to study the loose threads of the tattered and worn *welcome* rug placed strategically in front of Elizabeth's door.

Welcome.

Right.

Nerves wound me tight, a vise constricting the base of my throat. I fought to put up those walls of protection, desperate to guard my heart against what I would find inside.

For three months it'd been like this. But there was no getting used to it. I mean, God, I hadn't gotten over Elizabeth in those six years I'd been away. There had been absolutely nothing I could do to cover up the love I had for her, no desires or goals or bodies dense enough to bury the need that had consumed me since the first time I'd glimpsed her. She'd stolen something from me that I'd never gotten back, something she kept hidden deep beneath the surface in places I doubted either of us could see, in places neither of us could define.

Did I really think I'd be able to strip her from my spirit now?

Metal scraped as the deadbolt was set free. The door slowly swung open to reveal Elizabeth standing there.

Unable to stop myself, my eyes sought out the *one*. The one who owned me, heart and soul. Looking at her crushed me anew. It was a punch straight to the gut, hard enough to knock the air from my lungs.

No. There wasn't a chance in hell I would ever stop loving this woman.

She was thin. Too thin, her cheeks sunken and her arms frail, her skin ashen and pale. But it was the warmth that had been snubbed from her eyes that absolutely killed me.

Broken.

There was no other way to describe her.

Every part of me ached to step across the threshold, to take her in my arms and promise her that I would somehow help her heal, that in time, it really would be okay, and that one day, it wouldn't hurt so bad.

But I had no fucking idea how to gather the scattered pieces, no clue how to put her back together.

For a fleeting moment, my eyes locked with hers, and I thought maybe I glimpsed it, a transient flicker of her own longing, like maybe she was wishing I was strong enough to save her, too.

In clear discomfort, Elizabeth dropped her gaze

and fidgeted as she looked to the floor. "Lizzie, honey." Her voice was weak. "Your daddy is here."

"Coming!" Lizzie called back from upstairs. The muted echoes of my child's movements in her room above filtered down to where I waited for her in the entryway below.

I shifted in the unease, attempting to study Elizabeth from where I pretended my focus was on my shoes. Gauging her, I tried to get some sense of whether she was really okay.

What a ridiculous notion. *Okay*. What did that even mean? Because okay in itself seemed impossible. Unattainable. She was most definitely not okay.

Fuck.

And neither was I. Not even close.

I knew she could feel me, the severity of my hidden stare, even when I was doing my best to conceal it beneath the suffocating tension that ricocheted between us every single time we were in the other's presence. She tucked her chin deeper as if she could deflect my concern, curled and clenched her hands.

God, seeing her engagement ring on her left hand killed me.

I wanted to shake her. To beg her to snap out of it.

To plead with her to open her eyes and *see*. To remember exactly why she'd allowed me to place that ring there in the first place. I wanted to demand to know why she didn't take it off.

But me pushing her was exactly what had cast the fatal stone, what had driven the last nail into splintering wood. The fracture between us was so profound, the pressure so intense, there was nothing we could do to stop the break. A separation of hearts when they just wouldn't hold.

My gaze jerked upward when I heard footsteps above. Lizzie ran out of her room. She bounded downstairs, her inky black hair set free. Soft wisps and bangs framed that precious face. Her backpack bounced on her shoulders with each urgent step.

The pain in my heart ebbed. Just a fraction. But it was there.

This little girl was my light.

She smiled when she hit the last stair and hopped down into the foyer.

"Morning, Daddy." She smiled through her haste.

"Good morning, princess. How's my baby girl this morning?"

"I'm good, Daddy. I'm all ready for school and my backpack is all full, too," she said with a distinct sense of pride and a resolute nod of her head.

"How about your lunch, sweetheart?" Elizabeth asked.

"I already packed it, Mommy. I'm all ready to

go."

"Well, I do believe you're forgetting something, Lizzie," I said, forcing myself to find a smile, to continue to show her how much I loved her.

Lizzie frowned, her little nose scrunched up in question. "What?"

"My hug, you silly girl."

A roll of giggles escaped her, and she rushed in to hug me around the waist. I wrapped my arms around her shoulders, leaned down to bury my nose in her hair, breathed her in.

When she started first grade a few weeks ago, she told me she was *too big* for me to hold her anymore.

God, did I ever disagree.

All I wanted was to pick her up so I could feel the weight of my daughter in my arms.

The way she was squeezing me now, I thought maybe she was feeling the same way, too.

"I missed you so much, Daddy," she finally whispered, all the levity from before gone, replaced with the gravity of our situation.

"I missed you, too, sweetheart. More than you could ever know."

She'd matured so much. The child had to have grown at least three inches over the summer. But where that maturity was really noticeable was in her expressions. Her cheekbones were becoming more prominent as the soft roundness of her chubby cheeks slowly faded away, as that baby face gave way to a little girl's.

And her eyes. The vast innocence that had swum in their depths had been erased in time, wiped out by circumstances no child should ever have to face.

"I think I'm going to need one of those, too, Lizzie," Elizabeth said with a tip of her head. Her smile was as forced as mine.

When we were with Lizzie, Elizabeth and I did our best to pretend as if everything was fine. It was the worst kind of deceit. The child had been affected just as severely as we had been, even if she hadn't been able to fully grasp the meaning. She only knew that the life we'd finally attained had been destroyed, that for six weeks, there'd been so much torment filling the walls of this little house, none of us could breathe.

And then she'd known her daddy had *left*.

Her sixth birthday had come with such joy. We had a party just as big as the one I first attended the year before, although this one had been without all the unease and tension that tarnished her fifth birthday party. None of that had existed on her sixth. Our family had been whole. Complete.

A week later, the security she found within the walls of that home had been crushed.

There was no doubt all of this had rocked her.

I glanced at the delicate gold ring she wore around her finger, the one Elizabeth and I had given her the night after I'd proposed to Elizabeth.

The commitment we had made to Lizzie was one we refused to break. No matter what happened between us, Lizzie would always know she was adored by both her mother and father. There was no fighting whether Lizzie would still be a part of my life. It'd come without question.

Now, it was just Elizabeth and I floundering, trying to figure out how to make all of this work.

Work.

Agony constricted every cell in my body, as if the life were being squeezed out of me, a slow asphyxiation. It was hard to comprehend how much standing here truly hurt. Physically. Mentally. Emotionally. It was excruciating.

Nothing about this *worked.*

We were barely surviving, just fumbling through the days.

And all of them were spent missing my girls.

Lizzie turned and mashed herself to Elizabeth. Elizabeth ran her fingers through Lizzie's hair and placed a tender kiss on the crown of her head.

"I'll be there to pick you up after school," she promised as she stepped back to free Lizzie from her hold.

"Okay, Mommy."

I rubbed at the sore spot on my chest, wishing

there was some way to soothe it. Hide it. Cover it. But there was no relief found in this miserable situation. How could there be? Because all I wanted were the two girls standing in front of me, and having only one of them for meager minutes a day did nothing to fill up the aching void.

Picking Lizzie up every morning for school took me to my highest high while it simultaneously knocked me to my lowest low.

Those precious moments with her were the only thing in this lonely life that I cherished. But leaving her there at the school entrance, watching her hair swish along her back as she disappeared through the gate, was the worst kind of reminder of what I was missing.

Warily, I glanced at Elizabeth. The woman I loved. The one who wouldn't even spare me a glance.

I swallowed the lump in my throat. "We'd better get going or you'll be late for school," I coaxed as I brushed my fingers along Lizzie's shoulder.

She nodded, the sweet smile making a resurgence. It was as if the child didn't know how to act, the joy that lived deep within her, that natural goodness vying to make its way out while the sorrow that had taken over our lives fought to keep it down.

"Bye, Mommy," she called behind her as she turned and walked away.

I took her hand and led her down the sidewalk. The door quietly clicked shut behind us.

Lizzie climbed into her spot in the backseat of my car, tossing her backpack onto the seat beside her before she buckled herself into her booster.

I situated myself in the driver's seat, put my car in reverse, and glanced at my little girl through the rearview mirror as I backed out of the driveway.

I hadn't seen her since I'd dropped her back at her mother's on Saturday morning after she spent Friday night with me at my condo. The weekends without Lizzie were the worst.

"How was your weekend, princess?"

Lizzie shrugged a little and trained her attention out the window. "Okay, I guess," she said, her voice low, woven with despondence.

I put the car in drive and headed toward her school. Maybe it was completely out of the way, an irrational chore to travel all this way to drive her a mile to her school every morning. I didn't care. I needed this time with her, this connection that promised I was still an integral part of her life.

"Just okay?" I prodded, struggling to keep my voice from cracking. I hated seeing her this way. Her mood constantly fluctuated, up and down, back and forth, hints of my sweet baby girl emerging then receding just as quickly.

"I was just bored. Uncle Maffew and Auntie Natalie didn't come over all weekend, and Mommy didn't want to go to the beach," she almost pouted. She paused, grimaced as she continued on, seemingly grasping for the good things that did transpire over the days we'd been apart. "Mommy did play with me a little bit, but then she got tired and took a nap. And she let me pick out dinner and I helped her make it, too." She smiled a little as her attention flitted up to meet mine in the mirror. "I got lots of time to play with my new dolls you got me, Daddy. And I got my dollhouse all set up."

We'd gone shopping Friday night, searching out a dining room set for her prized dollhouse that was tucked in the corner of her room. We'd ended up with a tiny dining room set, and I couldn't say no when Lizzie had asked me to add two new members to the ever-growing miniature family. Lately Lizzie seemed to spend more time lost in the sanctuary of their world than in her own.

Sorrow swamped me, because I could feel my daughter's own. I hated it. I would do anything to be able to take it away.

"That doesn't sound so bad." I made a feeble attempt at encouraging her.

She sighed, slumped her chin in her hand as she rested her forehead on the window, her attention focused on the blur of the passing street. "I just don't know why you can't sleep at our house. It's better when you're there, Daddy."

Her words cut right through me. I fought to gather myself, to keep it under control, because I knew I had to stay strong for my little girl.

I forced myself to speak. "We already talked about why I can't right now."

The problem was all of those reasons had come with little conviction. I didn't believe them myself.

"Just tell Mommy you're sorry," she begged quietly. I heard the tears building in the vulnerability that wound its way into her angel voice.

God.

How was I going to get through another conversation like this? We had them often, and I'd give just about anything to offer her a different answer, to come up with a different result.

I wanted one myself.

Sighing heavily, I scrubbed my palm over my face, blinked as I tried to focus ahead through the sorrowful haze that clouded my vision.

"It's not that simple, Lizzie." God, how much did I wish it was.

Silence hovered in the car before she finally spoke again. "Your voice was so loud, Daddy. You made Mommy cry." Her words came as a whisper, a memory that so clearly traumatized my little girl.

That day had been the first emotion I'd seen from Elizabeth in weeks. It'd been charged, the moment when Elizabeth had finally broken and I'd cracked.

I'd said things I never should have.

But Elizabeth had said them, too.

"I hate that you heard that, Lizzie, but sometimes grown-ups have fights and we raise our voices. None of that was directed at you."

"But then you *left*," she countered. "You're supposed to say you're sorry when you do something bad."

Palpitations fluttered my heart. The deepest sense of grief and a suggestion of awe took hold. My little girl forever grasped so much more than I imagined she did. The intuitiveness that always seemed veiled beneath her child-like naivety shone through with the wise, logical words that she spoke.

If only it were that easy.

"Your mom and I are doing the best we can right now, sweetheart. But no matter what, we love you more than anything. You know that, don't you?"

Intense blue eyes met mine in the mirror, honest and pure. "I always know that, Daddy. It just makes me sad that you can't stay."

Relief assuaged some of the guilt that wouldn't let go, and a wistful smile pulled at my mouth. "You're an amazing child, Little Elizabeth."

Lizzie blushed the brightest red and fought a grin. Dimples dented her cheeks.

Affection pushed at my ribs.

I rarely called her that, but sometimes, I just couldn't help myself.

She bore little physical resemblance to her mother, but I glimpsed her in so many things, the child a striking reminder of a young Elizabeth.

Sweet and kind.

Timid and shy and incredibly confident in the exact same moment.

Wise, but continuously led by her emotions.

Good.

That, and she shared Elizabeth's grandmother's name.

"I like that name, Daddy," she mumbled through her shyness, that sweet little girl back again.

"I do, too, princess," I whispered to her, emotion cresting my mouth. I loved her so much, so much it hurt.

She smiled a little. A silent conversation passed between us, something that spoke of a deep understanding. On some level, my little girl recognized what I was going through and the way I truly felt. She knew I would go home to them if I could, that if I could break down Elizabeth's walls, I would.

I made a left-hand turn and merged right to wind into the circular drop-off in front of Lizzie's school.

"Look!" Lizzie suddenly squealed.

I craned my head to try to take in what had caused such a reaction in Lizzie, the child overflowing with excitement. As I came to a full stop at the curb, she quickly unbuckled and shot forward in her seat. She pointed out to the sidewalk.

"What is it?" I asked, my eyes scanning the sea of children jumping from backseats of cars, slinging backpacks onto their shoulders, yelling and laughing as they began their day.

"Daddy, look it...right there!" She jabbed her finger in emphasis, and my sight finally settled on the source of the furor that surged through Lizzie.

A wistful smile emerged on my face.

Kelsey Glenn.

She stood on the sidewalk with her father, Logan. He knelt on a knee in front of her, helping her secure her backpack onto her shoulders. The little girl grinned as her dad lightly nudged her chin with the hook of his finger.

I'd met her a handful of times. Over the summer, the two girls had become close friends. I thought it was cute that Lizzie finally had a playmate that she gushed about almost every time I saw her, the way Lizzie would worry if Kelsey would like something or not, going on about Kelsey's favorite food or favorite color or favorite show.

There was nothing that gave me mixed feelings like watching Lizzie grow up, to see her excited to have friends, to talk on the phone and giggle like a teenager. She was only six, but the last year had passed in what seemed a blink, a blip of time that now flickered and held as memories in my consciousness. I knew that as the years passed, they would only quicken. Lizzie would be grown before I could make sense of it.

It made me proud and sad, ushering in a fearful expectancy of what the future would bring.

Kelsey spent her time living between her parents' houses, carted between the two on whichever day belonged to her mother or father. The two girls had been in the same kindergarten class. As the school year had neared its ending, right before everything had fallen apart, Elizabeth had found out her father lived just two streets over from us, and Lizzie and Kelsey had clung to each other over the difficult months that had ensued.

I guess I'd never thought it possible that Kelsey and Lizzie would end up having so much in common.

Lizzie couldn't stop talking about her.

"What's her name again...Kelly...Katie...Karen?" I teased.

"Daddy..." Lizzie drew out in a frustrated groan. "It's Kelsey. And she's my very best friend. Didn't you know that? She even gave me a necklace that says so."

I grinned as I peeked at my daughter in the rearview mirror. She played with the little pendant necklace she proudly wore around her neck. She lifted it a little higher when she caught my eye.

"See!" she prodded.

"Well, it looks like it's official then."

"Yep." She giggled a little.

The sound filled the car, filled my heart. It felt so good to hear her laugh. For so long, it'd been missing. And I knew even if Elizabeth and I never healed from this, our daughter would.

"Well, we better get you out of here so you can catch up with her."

I came around to the rear passenger side and opened the door. Lizzie slid out onto the safety of the walkway and grabbed her backpack from the seat. She slammed the door shut behind her.

Dropping to a knee, I helped her slide her backpack straps up her arms, then pulled her hair free from underneath it.

Softly I smiled at her, my attention locked on the sweetness in her vibrant blue eyes.

"You have a great day today, okay? I'm going to be thinking about you all day and all night until I see you again tomorrow morning. Then you're going to come and spend tomorrow night with me. Does that sound like a good plan?"

She smiled a little. "Yeah, Daddy, I like that

idea."

"Lizzie!" The peal of a high-pitched voice reverberated across the lot. "Lizzie, over here!"

We both jerked to see Kelsey running our direction, the biggest grin on her face. The little girl smiled up at me as she approached. "Hi, Mr. Davison. Is it okay if Lizzie walks with me to class?"

"That's fine by me."

Lizzie beamed as she squinted up at me, every trace of her earlier melancholy erased. "Thank you, Daddy! I'll see you tomorrow."

I dropped a quick kiss to her forehead. "Bye, sweetheart. You be good. I'll call you tonight."

"Okay!" she said as the two turned. Giggles rolled from them both as they shot off in the direction of the school gates.

Logan casually walked up, wearing a pair of cargo shorts and a tee-shirt. He shoved his hands in his pockets. "Morning."

"Morning," I returned absently, my attention on the two little girls skipping up the sidewalk.

"They sure are cute together, aren't they?" he mused.

"Yeah." They really were.

"Kelsey can't stop talking about Lizzie," he continued. "She asks if Lizzie can come over and play just about every time she's at my house."

"Yeah?" I said, the word not really a question,

but a filler to take up the time that passed until my daughter disappeared into the mass of students flooding into the school hall.

"Elizabeth looked a lot better last week when I picked Kelsey up over there. I was glad to see a little color in her face."

A deep frown burrowed in my brow as I cast a suspicious glance his way.

He was looking forward, watching the girls. His body was relaxed, chunks of his light blond hair stirred up by the short gusts of wind. But he was working his jaw. Nervous. Agitated.

Awareness prickled along my senses like a solitary string that pulled at my consciousness. A warning flare.

This asshole was digging. Waiting. Wanting.

The anger that had smoldered for all those months boiled, rose up in a swollen rage.

Did he think for one fucking second I'd let him have her? That I'd stand aside and watch the woman I'd loved for all my life fully slip from my grasp?

Yeah. Maybe I'd lost her. But that didn't mean I was letting her go.

He looked over at me. Flinty green eyes narrowed as they took in my expression. He lifted his chin.

"I'll see you around." Then he turned and headed back toward his car. He pitched a fleeting glance at me from over his shoulder before he climbed into his car.

The sharpest shot of possessiveness rattled me straight to the core, deep enough to cut into the compulsory resignation that had spurred me to pack my things and walk out of Elizabeth's house.

He pulled from the curb and out into the swarm of merging and exiting cars. He caught the severity of my gaze as I followed his departure. There wasn't a god-damned thing I could do to stop myself from staring him down.

Because it slammed me—the realization that just because Elizabeth couldn't stomach the sight of me didn't mean she might not one day want someone else.

My hands curled into the tightest fists, and I buried them in the pockets of my slacks, struggling to hang onto my last ounce of sanity because I knew I was about five seconds from losing my fucking mind.

I just wasn't rational when it came to her.

She was mine.

She'd always been.

And I was going to make sure she always was.

four

Distorted, late afternoon light diffused through the small, glazed window, tossing muted beams of sunlight across Elizabeth's alcove bathroom. They struck the floor in slanted rays and lit up the dense motes that floated, suspended in the air. The walls felt as if they were closing in, and it was quiet. So damned quiet.

I paced the floor. My footsteps echoed back my impatience. What else was I supposed to do?

These had to be the longest three minutes of my life.

I raked two restless hands though my hair. My fingers dug into my skin and scraped along my scalp. Gripping the back of my neck, I turned my face to the ceiling and exhaled, hoping to release some of the pent-up pressure I couldn't seem to expel from my body.

God, I couldn't take this.

"Would you stop? You're making me nervous." Elizabeth fidgeted from her spot where she was propped up against the bathroom counter. She glanced at me askew. The tiniest of smiles played at her mouth. It tugged at those places inside me that only existed with her, simply because in her, they'd been created.

One side of my mouth lifted in a soft curl of affection. Her blonde hair was piled in a messy twist on her head, and a misshapen sweatshirt fell off one shoulder, the perfect partner to the pair of thin, black leggings she wore. Standing there, she looked so much like the eighteen-year-old girl I'd first met rather than the twenty-seven-year-old woman she was.

God, she was a vision, perfection in my eyes.

It was her expression that loosened that ball of anxiety knotting me tight. She looked up at me in anticipation, with trust and hope and the same excitement that was just about to fry my nerves.

I drew in a calming breath.

She was late. Just one day. But that didn't

matter. I think both of us already knew. We could feel our lives teetering on the cusp of change. The only thing left now was begging that little stick to put to rest the uncertainty, to give us its promise, to tell us that this was really happening.

Elizabeth stretched out her hand and silently beckoned me to her. That smile she wore on her beautiful face grew a little, nervously fluttering around the edges.

How could any one woman affect me this way? How could her touch both burn me and soothe me in the same simple stroke?

A smile teetered at my mouth as I slipped up in front of her. I gently wound her in my arms, and she laid her head on my chest. Little tremors rolled the length of her body.

"You're shaking," I murmured, running my fingers through her hair, hoping to calm her.

She edged back a fraction. Between us, she placed both hands flat across her belly. She looked up at me from beneath her lashes, her eyes all alight and alive.

"I'm not shaking." Her voice dropped low, and she whispered her awe. "It's butterflies."

A sharp exhale escaped through my nose. There was no fear hiding below the surface of her words, no remnants of distrust spinning though her spirit. Nothing here threatened to take us back to that day. This…this was the way it should have been, how I should have been, standing there supporting the one who meant everything.

I ran my thumb across the sharp angle of her cheekbone. "Butterflies, huh?"

"Yeah," she answered, chancing a hopeful grin. Warmth gleamed in her soft brown eyes.

Somehow Elizabeth managed to undo me a little more.

"Does that mean you already know what that test is going to say?" And I thought I did, too, thought I could feel it. Maybe I'd convinced myself into believing something just because I wanted it so badly. I didn't know. But damn, if I didn't ever want this.

Things were crazy with the wedding plans. It was hard to believe we'd gotten home from New York less than a month ago. We'd announced to Elizabeth's family our plans, that we were actually setting a date.

June seventh.

God, it seemed impossible to fathom that things were finally as they should be.

Just five short months and Elizabeth would be mine, completely.

Natalie and Elizabeth's sisters had immediately set to work on wedding plans, fretting over this day that, in my eyes, couldn't be anything less than perfect simply because Elizabeth would become my wife.

It didn't matter the place or the food or what everyone would wear.

All that mattered were the vows we were going to make.

Our lives had transformed so drastically in such a short period of time. We hadn't been trying for this, but thought we'd just let it take its course. I mean, things were already chaotic, a disorganized mayhem, both of our houses on the market as we searched for a home to fill with love and the memories of our lives, plus the constant wedding plans we were running around organizing. But it was a welcomed mayhem.

I had a feeling it was about to get worse.

Seeming to get lost in thought, Elizabeth let her attention travel to the far wall. A few seconds later, she turned the force of it back on me.

"I didn't think this would happen so fast. I'm not sure why, but I thought we'd have to work for it. But this…" Earnestly she pressed her hands more firmly to her stomach. "This blessing…I've been pretty sure of it for the last week. I just…know."

I cupped her cheek. My attention flitted over every line and curve of the face forever burned in my mind. "I can't wait to do this with you."

She smiled up at me. A faint blush tinted her cheeks and tears glistened in her eyes. "I really hope we're not getting ahead of ourselves."

Longing rushed from her in waves. Each one crashed into me, as if some unconscious part of her were begging me to make this real.

I wanted so badly to give it to her.

"If not today, then we will celebrate it on another. But we will do this together, Elizabeth."

She nodded against my palm and brought hers up to cover mine. She wrapped her fingers around mine. "Thank you for being here, Christian. For sharing this moment with me...whatever direction it goes."

On the counter, the timer dinged.

I lay my cheek against hers, let her warmth surround me. My hold was secure. I was there for her one way or another. Even if this didn't turn out the way we wanted it, we'd deal with it.

"You ready?" I asked.

She blinked. "So ready."

Her message was clear, rang in my ears and in my heart, a promise that every question of my devotion to her had been erased from her mind.

She clung to me as we turned our faces to the test sitting beside us on the bathroom counter.

I felt her lose her breath, and I wound my arms around her a little tighter to hold her up as her legs weakened beneath her.

Two pink lines.

This time, there was no question she was shaking. She trembled in my arms. "Christian," fell as a breath from her mouth, bled into the room as wonder and awe.

Two pink lines.

There was no greater joy than what I felt in this moment. It just didn't exist. Nothing else could compare.

She was crying as I knelt on the floor in front of her. I wrapped my hands around her waist, buried my face in her stomach where our child grew. Where a new life had begun.

I was overcome.

Elizabeth gentled her fingers through my hair. I tipped my head back so I could look at her. I slipped my hands to the outside of her waist in the same second she took my face in her hands.

"We're going to have a baby, Christian," she said.

Saying it aloud seemed to rip something open inside of her. She choked over a cry that spoke of so many things—shock and relief and joy, crushing the vestiges of disbelief that had lingered in these walls.

"A baby," she whispered again through a fervent sob. "Oh my God, Christian... I don't know how to explain what I'm feeling right now. How happy I am. I didn't think I'd ever get to have this again. I'd accepted that it was only ever going to be me and Lizzie." Passion poured from her mouth, her spirit seeking understanding in mine.

"I…I…" She stumbled over her thoughts, wet her lips as she looked at me through bleary eyes. "You know, you're the only one I've ever wanted this with…the only one I'd ever give this to. Thank you for finding me, for loving me, for filling up the void in my life…for giving me this."

"God, Elizabeth…"

How could I respond to that when I'd been the one to leave that void in the first place? But I knew…knew I was the only one who fit in that void, because it was Elizabeth that perfectly filled mine, too. "Nothing in this world could make me happier than this," I urged.

Unchecked tears streamed down her face, and she took me by the hands and held them flat at her stomach.

I swallowed over the lump wedged at the base of my throat, my hands burning into her flat stomach that would soon grow round.

In the fading light of the room, we held our child.

My mind raced with images of what was taking hold in the deepest places of Elizabeth's body.

Was this a boy or girl?

I wondered if again the child would take after me the way Lizzie did? Maybe have a tiny cleft like the one Lizzie wore on her chin and the same shock of black hair on her head? Would he watch the world through intuitive, blue eyes, just like

Lizzie?

Or would she be a small Elizabeth, would her eyes be warm and brown, would blonde curls frame her face, would her heart go on in unending innocence, kindness, and compassion?

Or would this child defy the imaginable?

"I'm so happy, Elizabeth," I whispered at her stomach, hoping that maybe this child could sense the devotion flooding from us, the love we had already found ourselves in.

I'd forever regret not being there for Lizzie. Even though my spirit had recognized her the second I saw her, the truth was, I'd only known my little girl for a matter of months. But somehow, somewhere in the bleakness of that time, she had still made her mark on my heart. Through time and space, she'd managed to touch me. She had stirred something in me that I never wholly understood until the moment I first saw her.

I shouldn't have been surprised that this child already had, too.

A smile washed the entirety of Elizabeth's face, those same images I'd been thinking of before so obviously playing behind her eyes.

Then she offered a soggy grin. "Lizzie is going to be the best big sister. I can't wait to tell her."

"I can't imagine a better big sister." I smiled up at her, running my hands up her stomach then wrapping them firmly around her waist. I tugged her a little, rocked her forward.

Her hands fell to my shoulders for support and a tiny giggle of surprise rolled from her mouth. She raked her bottom lip between her teeth.

God, she was always pushing me to the edge of sanity, driving me a little mad because only this girl could stir these impossible things in me, wind me up and tie me from the inside out. In the same pass of her hand, she managed to put me at the greatest ease.

She was what made me complete. She was what made me right.

"How'd we get this lucky, Elizabeth?"

She touched my face and slowly shook her head. "I have no idea…but I'm not going to let it go."

***

TWO WEEKS LATER

Elizabeth was on her knees on the bathroom floor. For what had to have been the tenth time in the last thirty minutes, she vomited. Her entire body trembled and shook as she purged the contents of her stomach into the toilet. She squeezed her eyes shut, her back arching as she lifted up higher on her knees and gasped for a breath.

I swept back the hair matted to her forehead, lifted it from her neck that was drenched with sweat.

God, this was complete torture. I didn't think I'd ever felt so helpless in my life. All I wanted was to fix her, to make her better, to take it away.

And I couldn't do a goddamned thing.

She gulped for air before she lurched forward and heaved again. This time, nothing came up. An indistinct whine fumbled from her mouth as her muscles clenched and strained, and she gripped the edge of the toilet as her body fought to expel something that just wasn't there.

With a heavy sigh, I placed a kiss to her temple. "Hold on a second."

Harshly she nodded, and I climbed to my feet. Grabbing a washcloth from the linen closet, I ran it under cool water and wrung it out. My footsteps were subdued as I shuffled back to her.

I knelt down beside her. "Here," I whispered, wishing to find anything that would soothe her, even in the slightest way.

She felt miserable, and it caused me physical pain to see it.

That pain contorted my face with sympathy when I hooked my index finger under her chin and drew her face toward me.

Shit.

She looked awful…and beautiful.

How was that even possible?

I swept the cloth over the moisture gathered on

her brow. Elizabeth whimpered, and her eyes fell closed as she allowed me to take care of her. I dabbed the cloth gently at the chapped skin of her lips.

"I hate that you're going through this," I murmured as I flipped the cloth around and ran it over the back of her neck.

For a moment she sagged, a moment's reprieve, before another roll of nausea hit her. She pitched forward. She strained, every muscle in her body stretched thin, her stomach constricting as she gagged. Nothing came up except for the agonized moan that tore from her throat. A stream of tears slicked down her face, cries she couldn't contain.

I brushed the bangs from her face and placed a supporting hand at the base of her head. "Is there anything I can do?"

She swallowed hard. Her voice was all raspy, like maybe it was hard just to speak. "Just don't leave me."

A smile fluttered at my mouth, and my thumb caressed the soft skin of her cheek. "I'm not going anywhere, baby."

I'd barely left her side in two days. I'd stood, or rather knelt beside her, when the effects of the pregnancy had suddenly taken hold. It'd seemed almost a shock because, two nights ago, we'd gone to sleep with her feeling completely fine—feeling good was what she'd said—and it wasn't four hours later that she'd jumped out of bed in the early hours of the morning. Shocked from sleep and gripped by fear, I fumbled out of the tangled sheets and rushed into the bathroom where I found her on the floor, her body sick with the strain the child growing within her caused.

In the last two days, it hadn't let up.

Honestly, it scared me, watching her suffer this way. In the few minutes I'd found to sneak away, I'd been on my phone, researching if this was normal, and if it was, what we could do about it.

Of course, there was no shortage of suggestions, a mess of folklore and superstition that I wasn't about to test out on my future wife. Dotted in between were the few remedies that possibly seemed legitimate.

But basically, we had to wait it out.

She frowned. "Don't look at me like that."

I felt one form in return. "How am I looking at you?"

She almost smiled. "Like if I throw up one more time, you might have a meltdown."

I chuckled lightly. "That obvious, huh?"

This time, she managed a smile, and she wiped the back of her hand across her mouth. "It's really not as bad this time, Christian," she mumbled in what I could only assume was supposed to be some kind of reassurance.

It did nothing to allay my concern, only

inflamed the residual guilt that would haunt me for the rest of my life.

Seeing her like this brought so much to light, uncovered all those things that I'd never borne witness to, things buried in the unknowns of Elizabeth's life when I'd been absent.

Yeah, I had a vague sense of what she'd gone through. She'd described it, but when a person isn't there to witness suffering, it's hard to comprehend it. But to cause her to quit school, I knew it had to have been bad. That knowledge had been a huge blow to me, struck me deep and beat me down. I mean, God, I'd left her alone to go through all of that by herself.

The truth was, though, I really didn't know what she'd suffered. I just had no clue.

Now I was getting the idea.

Elizabeth's eyes went wide, and she jerked back to the toilet. Her knees dug into the floor as she held herself up. She strained and moaned and begged for something to give.

My heart hurt a little more.

God, this was awful.

But not for a second did Elizabeth complain. She just took it in stride, attributed it to something her body required of her in return for the child it protected.

I would never cease to be amazed by her.

"I'm going to run downstairs to get you some

water. Will you be okay while I'm gone?"

"Yeah, I'll be fine."

"Do you need anything else? Crackers or something?"

So maybe crackers were about the only thing I'd seen on my search that I'd be inclined to suggest Elizabeth put in her body. I wasn't willing to take the chance—not on her or the baby.

"No, I'm okay."

I hesitated.

"Honestly, Christian…I've been through this before."

Nodding, I turned and rushed downstairs, led by the muted nightlights Elizabeth had set up for Lizzie in case she woke up in the middle of the night.

In the kitchen, I grabbed a glass from the cupboard and filled it with cool water. An uncontainable yawn escaped me. Exhaustion threatened. On instinct, my gaze traveled to the clock on the microwave that taunted me with the sleep we'd lost. It was almost three.

"Shit," I muttered. Hoping to wake myself up, I scrubbed a palm over my face and dragged myself back upstairs.

But how could I complain?

I couldn't.

There was nothing here for me to complain about. Nothing but my worry for Elizabeth. She was the one who had to endure this.

So what if I lost a few hours' sleep. I could deal. I sure as hell wasn't about to leave Elizabeth to suffer through this alone.

Not again.

Not a chance.

At the bathroom doorway, I paused when I found Elizabeth in the same position I'd left her in. Exhaling heavily, I eased up behind her and dropped to my knees at her side. I ran a soothing hand up the length of her spine and to her neck, softly tilting her face toward me.

"Here, baby, drink a little of this."

She searched for the strength to smile, allowed me to lift the glass to her dry, cracked lips. If we weren't careful, she'd end up dehydrated.

She took the smallest of sips and closed her eyes as she forced it down. For a moment, she remained still, as if she were testing the reaction, assessing if she could keep it down. Slowly her eyelids fluttered open. She whispered her thanks.

My head slanted in sincerity. "Don't thank me, Elizabeth. I'm in this with you."

Somewhere inside her, she found the energy to bait me with the hint of a tease. "You are, huh?"

Her efforts came out weak.

Gentle, sympathetic laughter quietly tumbled from my mouth, and I was unable to keep the playful buzz from lighting in my chest. A deep sense of wonder hit me. This girl could even rib me when she was at her worst.

"One-hundred percent," I said.

She gestured with her chin toward the toilet. "So, do you think you could take this over for me?"

I pushed back the chunk of hair that had fallen into her beautiful face and wound it with my finger. An unrestrained smile split my face. At my reaction, her warm eyes swam with emotion, so thick, so pure, so…good. Softening, I tucked the matted tuft of blonde behind her ear and trailed my knuckles down her jaw.

"You know I would if I could."

Elizabeth grasped my wrist, pressed my palm to her face as if it were her lifeline. "I know you would."

She held me there for the longest time, the air between us full, both alive and subdued, a quiet comfort we fell into. Her eyes dimmed before they fell closed. "I'm so tired," she admitted.

"Come here." I shifted and leaned up against the tub, my legs stretched out in front of me. I cringed a little when my bare back met the cold porcelain surface. A shiver slipped down my spine, but I shook it off and pulled Elizabeth to me. She curled into my side and rested her head on my chest, nuzzled and nestled until she found a comfortable spot.

I wrapped her in my arms. Her skin was cool to the touch, clammy, sticky with sweat.

I brought my mouth to the top of her head and kissed her there, murmured out a promise I'd be sure to keep. "You're going to be okay, Elizabeth."

She snuggled deeper and turned just enough to place a tender kiss to the center of my chest. "Only because you're here."

five

The door quietly latched shut behind me, and I slumped against it for support as I squeezed my eyes closed, praying…praying for it to end.

I didn't know how much longer I could do this. Didn't know how much more I could take.

I fought the weakness that trembled my knees, because I didn't want to be this woman. I hated her. I didn't recognize her.

But I didn't know how to make her go away.

My stomach curled. Nausea spun through my gut the same way it did every time I saw Christian's face, a tumultuous chaos that wracked my senses, confused and clouded the truth that was lost somewhere inside me.

It was visceral. A reaction I couldn't stop. Each morning I begged for this to be the day when I opened the door and I would recognize myself. The day I would recognize Christian as the man I loved.

That I'd want him.

No one understood how desperately I wanted to.

None of them understood the way I really felt.

Clutching my chest, I gulped for air, begging for anything that would deaden this unyielding pain suffocating me from the inside out. Unbearable agony pressed and crushed, cutting deeper into the places where my life had been snubbed out, infiltrating the crevices of darkness where the light had been ripped from my soul.

It was blinding.

Excruciating.

Malignant.

And there was nothing I could do to stop it.

Hot, angry tears burned under my lids. Uncontrollably they fell, streaming from the creases of my pinched eyes. I lifted my face toward the ceiling, my head digging into the hard wood. I cried out, letting the pain that festered within me rip up my throat. I expelled my misery into the silence of the hollowed-out walls of this house. But the relentless desolation only echoed back the memories of what used to be my home. Those memories swallowed me whole.

At my chest, I fisted my hands in the shirt I'd worn for the last three days. "Help me," I whimpered.

But there was nothing that could save me. Nothing that could turn back time. Nothing that could give me back what I had lost.

Hopelessness had become my only partner.

I staggered out into the middle of the small family room where a week's worth of unfolded laundry was piled on the couch. There were so many good memories here. This tiny room was where Christian and I had found each other again. For months, it was here that we'd sat as we played with our daughter, as I'd slowly come to the realization that I had to have him a part of our lives. Part of my life.

How could I not see him in it now?

Something within me had been erased. Obliterated. Because I *knew* I loved him. I just couldn't feel it anymore.

Every time I witnessed the worry lining his face, it brought it all rushing back, and the only thing I wanted was to block it all out.

And I was so angry, so angry with him, and yet I didn't even know why.

I crammed my fists in my eyes, trying to push the mess of emotions that had surfaced back into the place where they belonged. Hidden.

Frantically wiping away my tears, I drew in a ragged breath. I grabbed onto the railing to hold myself upright as I staggered upstairs. I fell face-down into the unmade bed that Christian and I were supposed to share. I buried my face in the pillow and exhaled the air from my lungs as I wrapped my arms tightly around it.

I hated that I almost felt relieved. I loved my little girl so much, but forcing myself to find the energy to take care of her was the most difficult task I'd ever faced. I just wanted to sleep, and when she was at school or with Christian, that's what I did.

Deafening silence resounded in the room. I squeezed my eyes tighter, giving into the darkness that had somehow become my life.

Six

"Come here, you," Christian said as he reached for my hand. Night had fallen. Flames licked up, glowed and danced from the fireplace in the corner of the small family room, keeping out the slight chill that had taken hold outside. We'd tucked Lizzie in an hour earlier, and our daughter slept soundly upstairs. Christian was lying across the couch, and he tugged me down to him. I giggled as I crashed against his firm chest. He wrapped me in the security of his arms, and I snuggled into his warmth.

Gently he kissed the top of my head. His smile was uncontained as he nudged me up and kissed my nose. "You're on your feet too much," he scolded in the sweetest way. "You amaze me. Do you know that?"

Affection vibrated through my being.

It was he who amazed me.

I'd never felt more adored, more cherished, more loved.

Nonstop, Christian had taken care of me during the last few months. They'd been rough. Just like with Lizzie, sickness had gripped me morning and night. With his support, I'd done my best to get through it. I'd still taken care of my daughter and had continued to work at the bank, although I'd called in sick more times than I'd actually gone in.

But unlike with Lizzie, my sickness had slowly begun to fade once I hit the twelve-week mark.

Settling closer to him, I slipped between his side and the back of the couch. I rested my head in the crook of his shoulder. A contented sigh worked its way from me, and Christian hugged me a little tighter.

"How are you feeling tonight?" he murmured against my forehead.

"Good," I answered in all honesty. Well maybe not completely honest, because I didn't think I'd ever felt better than I did then. Maybe it was because I was so happy.

My fingers played along the collar of his white button-up before I brushed them up his neck and through the stubble that coated the sharp angle of his jaw. Touching him sent tingles rippling in the slowest wave, covering every inch of my body. I bit at my lip to hide my affected grin. Christian managed to make me feel things that shouldn't be possible, the softest brushes of skin igniting me through, setting me afire.

He tipped his head down so he could smile at me. "I'm so glad you're starting to feel a little better. It was killing me seeing you so miserable day after day."

I met his gaze. "I'd expected it to be that bad the entire time. And you know I would have happily gone through it, but I can't tell you how relieved I am that it's starting to go away. I'd been hoping this whole time I would feel well on our wedding and honeymoon."

It wasn't completely gone, not by any means. I still woke up and rushed to the bathroom every morning. But I could eat and I could work and I could easily make it through the day.

"Mmm…" His chest rumbled with the sexy sound, and the arm wound around my waist tightened its hold. "You'd better start saving your energy now." He raised a teasing, suggestive brow.

I laughed. "Oh, I'd better, huh?"

"Mmmhmm. You won't be getting any rest

during those two weeks."

Deep, penetrating bliss slipped through my veins, and this time, there was no concealing the smile that lit up my mouth. I could feel the force of it, the joy Christian brought me manifesting as a declaration on my face. Even with my expanding waist, Christian made me feel like I was the most desirable woman in the world. Like I was the center of his.

I no longer had any reservations believing it.

We settled into the comfort of the silence, and for the longest time, we just lay there wrapped up in each other. Christian ran his fingers through the length of my hair as I rested my head on his shoulder. Shadows danced and played across the ceiling, silhouettes twisting into unfathomable images that I only saw in my mind, flickers of imagined innuendo like glimpses into our future. The two of us seemed to get lost in it. Heat radiated from his skin, blanketing me, keeping me warm.

I'd be happy to stay in this spot forever.

Something deep had worked its way into Christian's consciousness, the severity of his thoughts almost palpable in the quiet of the room. He shifted farther to his side and laid me down on my back. His large hand came to rest on the tiny protuberance jutting out just below my belly button, his expression suddenly brimming with intensity.

My fingers fluttered up to his face, and I took in the serious lines etched deep at the corners of his eyes.

"What is it?" I whispered.

His throat bobbed as he swallowed deeply, and he turned away to look at the wall as he seemed to gather his thoughts. Then he locked his sharp gaze on me as he increased the pressure over the spot where our child rested.

"I just want to be a good father, Elizabeth. Sometimes it scares me that I don't know how." The words flowed like an admission, like a hidden worry that had plagued him, something old that had haunted him in the night. He stiffened. "I'm scared of what Lizzie's going to think once she really understands what I did. What's going to happen when she realizes her dad was a coward? That he left her mother when she needed him most? And what happens if I don't know how to show this baby how much love I have for her?"

Her.

It always brought a grin to me because he was so sure of it.

Even in the times when he wasn't so sure of himself.

We'd both taken to calling the child *her,* even though we wouldn't know for certain for another five weeks.

Everything in his expression was sincere. My eyes narrowed as I looked at him seriously. "Christian, you don't see what I see." What I'd seen since I'd finally allowed myself to believe. "Every time you look at our daughter, your devotion is clear. There is no question of it. Lizzie isn't going to question it, either. You're her hero. Just continue to love her the way you do. Be there for her when she needs you...show her the right way when she does something wrong, encourage her when she does something right."

My hand traveled down to cover Christian's where it was splayed wide across my stomach. "And this baby?" I pressed down in emphasis. "You've adored her since the second we found out."

God, Christian and I had fallen in love with this child. Upside down in love. He spent hours murmuring to her with his mouth pressed to my belly, the two of us cradling her together, much like we were doing now. And dreaming...dreaming of what she would look like, imagining the sound of her voice. Would she be quiet like Lizzie or stir our house into the perfect kind of frenzy?

But I guess we weren't prepared for how great our love really was on the morning we walked in for my first ultrasound three weeks ago at the twelve-week mark.

Seeing her for the first time...it'd jarred

something loose inside of me, a spot for her permanently carved into my spirit. And Christian... He'd been overcome. Undone. I was sure the man would never be the same.

"Do you really think there's any possibility she won't know how much you love her? There's no chance, Christian."

Blue eyes flashed the deepest emotion as he gripped me, palming the small bump that fit perfectly in his hand. "I love this child so much. Love my little Lizzie so much." He dipped down and kissed me, just the simplest brush of his lips, but still something that spoke of his passion. "God, I love you."

I ran my fingers up the planes of his chest and over his shoulders, couldn't look away from this gorgeous man whose presence filled up that void in me that had ached for so many years.

"Then you can't go wrong."

He slipped his hand up and spread his long fingers out over my chest, his fingertips ghosting along my collarbones. I could feel my heartbeat thrum steadily under them, his touch evoking a deep sense of security inside of me.

"What do you want to do, Elizabeth?"

Caught off guard by the abrupt shift in his tone, I frowned. "What do you mean?"

Christian tightened his hold, his grip like a vise as he locked himself to me. Intense. Almost demanding.

"I want to know what you want to do with your life. Do you want to go back to law school and become an attorney? Is that still what you want?" A harsh breath escaped him. "I can't stop thinking about all the times we talked when we were in college, all the dreams you had. You were going to save the world, Elizabeth, and I wanted to be there to watch you do it."

A wistful smile flitted the edges of my mouth as I thought of those days, the goals that had defined my life, because at the time, I'd believed them the most important aspect of who I'd become. But in the end, they weren't. Not even close.

"Those dreams fit into that period of my life, Christian. And when I lost them, a piece inside me was crushed. But when I look back now, I can't regret the way it turned out. I would never have been able to raise Lizzie the way I wanted to. Even working at the bank was challenging when she was little." I tilted my chin up to study him, tracing the sharp lines and angles of his face with my eyes. God, this man was beautiful. Breathtaking.

Inside and out.

Blue eyes blinked back at me, acute in their concern. It was so clear there, the vivid desire Christian had to reconcile the past, to make it right.

"Do you want to know what I really want?" I asked.

He cupped my cheek. "Anything, Elizabeth...anything you want, I want to give it to you."

A tremor of apprehension rolled through me. Not because of indecision. I wanted this. But some days it was still difficult to grasp that I didn't have to do it by myself anymore. I was no longer alone.

"I want to stay home. I want to be here when Lizzie gets off of school each day, and I don't want this baby to have to go to daycare. I know I told you before that I wanted to keep working, but now..." I sucked my bottom lip between my teeth and slowly shook my head. "I just want to be home to take care of my family, and if there's a way for me to do that, then that's truly what I want from my life."

I stared up at him hovering over me. Something that looked like respect shined down, his eyes shimmering with it.

He took my face in his hands. "Elizabeth, I will support you in whatever you want. If you want to stay home or if you want to go back to school, I will be here for you, and we will work it out. Hell, even if you want to continue working at the bank, then I want you to do that. But I can't think of anything better than knowing you are home with our kids."

Emotion thickened in my throat, a well of gratitude for this man who understood me better than anyone. I wet my lips. "This really is what I want."

He released a breath at my forehead. "Elizabeth, baby, we're going to do this, and we're going to do it right."

He tipped my chin up with the hook of his finger, his gaze washing over my face, his hold soft. Just as soft as the kiss he pressed to my lips. He deepened it, and I opened to him, welcomed the heat of his tongue as he swept it across mine.

Instantly, fire scorched through me.

Without breaking the kiss, Christian shifted and nudged my knees apart with one of his own. Gently he settled himself between my thighs. He urgently clutched the side of my face, his fingers trailing along my jaw, dipping into my hair, and running down my neck as he kissed me. Suspended a mere breath above me, his strong body pitched and lowered and teased, the lightest brushes and whispers that promised me what was to come.

I sighed into his mouth and let my fingers work into the rigid muscles of his back as he drowned me in the upsurge of his passion. He was gentle, so gentle, as if I might break, my fragile body safe in the security of his arms.

He groaned as he pulled back, his mouth at my jaw, nipping at my chin. "God, it's been too long since I've been inside you, Elizabeth." Rough, ragged words dropped from his mouth, his muscles ticking, twitching, begging for my touch.

I'd been so sick that I didn't think we'd made love but three or four times in the last few months.

And this...I wanted this. Needed this.

Christian grew hard and thick between us. The heavy weight of him rubbed against my belly. No question, the man needed this, too.

"Christian," I mumbled, yanking at the shirt tucked into his slacks. My palms found the bare skin of his back, and I flattened them against the sinewy muscle that rippled and twisted, jerking beneath my exploration. My grip demanding, I drew him nearer.

Did he have any idea how desperate I was to have him? How badly I needed him to possess me?

Christian hissed as I raked my nails down the smooth skin of his back to his narrow waist.

It would seem impossible, but just touching him seared me, scorching me in places that only existed with Christian. I trembled in anticipation. He intensified his kiss, forcing my surrender. His tongue played against mine. Desire pierced me when he sank his teeth into my lower lip.

A deep moan echoed through the sanctuary of the room, a sound I almost didn't recognize as it rolled from my tongue.

My head spun with his assault, and I found myself struggling to make sense of how much I loved this man. He was everything, beauty and light, my rock, the other piece of my soul.

And so incredibly beautiful. Sexy in every way. The fire in his blue eyes and strength of his body were something I would never get enough of. I would never get my fill, and the flame that he lit in the deepest places within me would never go dim.

He was my all.

"Shh…" he murmured, kissing me more as he lowered his onslaught, letting his hand flutter down my neck and glide to my breast.

His flicked his thumb over my nipple. Another shock of desire belted me and I moaned a little more. Christian inched back. Never breaking our kiss, his firm hands roamed down my sides, digging into my ribs before he grasped me by the hips. For one second, he severed our connection and glanced up toward the silence radiating from upstairs, then looked back on me with a cocky grin lifting just one side of his mouth.

"You need to be quiet because I'm going to take you right here, Elizabeth." His voice came low as he uttered the command close to my lips. He reached between us and jerked the button on my jeans free.

With his words, chills pebbled along my arms, lifted as a flush that rushed up my chest.

"Please," was all I could manage.

I was shaking as I blindly hurried through the buttons of his shirt. Christian edged back so I could get to the ones mashed between our chests, pressing both hands into the cushions on either side of my head.

He smirked against my mouth. "Are you anxious, Elizabeth?" he murmured, the question dripping from him as the slowest seduction. It vibrated through me.

"Yes," flooded from me as I pushed his shirt back from his shoulders.

The man had no idea.

He twisted out of his shirt, shaking one sleeve free from his wrist. He threw it to the floor and dove back for me as if I were his Promised Land.

My entire being hummed, relishing in his urgency as he flattened himself on top of me.

Guess he was anxious, too.

He kissed me until I was breathless, until I was panting and my heart was pounding, knocking at my ribs.

"Ugh...Christian," I begged. I lifted my hips. "Please...need you...need you," came as tiny pleas in between the desperate bid I made to get him closer, because I could never get him close enough.

I quaked as Christian slowly slid my shirt up and tugged it over my head. He tossed it to the floor on top of his and sat back on his knees and took me in.

Redness swept like wildfire just beneath the surface of my skin, heat and need and this passion

I held only for him rising up to tint my flesh.

I pressed my thighs into the outside of Christian's legs, squirming, loving when he looked at me this way, knowing my expression reflected exactly what I saw in his.

"Fuck, Elizabeth, do you have any idea what you do to me? Look at you," he said low as his gaze cut a path of fire over my body. His eyes flitted away from mine, his attention dropping to caress the black lace that covered my breasts and down my body to land on my waist.

Even the pass of his stare left a trail of chills in its wake.

Christian's tongue darted out to wet his lips, his agile fingers tugging at the waist of my jeans. He slipped off the couch and pulled them off, then made quick work of my panties and bra. Watching me, he unfastened the button of his slacks and slowly lowered his zipper. He pushed them down, stepping from his slacks and boxers, revealing every inch of this man's perfection. My eyes traveled his length. The lust that curled in my stomach sank, pooled as it throbbed between my legs.

Pulling the soft fleece blanket from the back of the couch, he flung it out and wrapped it around his shoulders. Slowly he slid back over me and completely draped us with it, the light fabric concealing us in its cover, enveloping us, our bodies and spirits caged.

I writhed.

Christian prodded my knees apart as he settled back over me, his face intense, the blue of his eyes all afire in this passion that would never let us go.

"I love you, Elizabeth," he whispered with his attention locked on mine.

In the same second, he locked his grip on the outside of my thigh. His erection slipped along my center, teasing, taunting, tempting.

"Love you more than you'll ever know," he said again as he tormented me, skimming his length along my folds.

Desire pulsed, coiled in my stomach and shook my legs. I whimpered, arching my back as I crushed my chest to his.

"I love you, Christian. Always. There is nothing that could make me stop loving you. Nothing that could make me stop needing you. You are my start and you are my finish, the one who's going to be there for everything in between." The words came as a solemn oath, my commitment to him.

Christian was my forever.

A pained smile edged his mouth as he held himself in restraint, his voice hoarse. "I will never let you go…never."

Heat sweltered between us, a fever of need building to a boil within the confines of the blanket, our bodies seeking, hunting for the other.

Above my head, Christian rigidly held himself up with his hand on the arm of the couch, the other digging deep into the flesh of my hip. He clenched his jaw as just the tip of his erection pressed into me.

"Fuck," he groaned, gritting his teeth. "It's been way to long."

I lifted my hips, taking more of him, but not enough. My fingertips dug into his shoulders, biting into his skin, imploring.

Christian dropped to his forearms, his face an inch from mine. "You," he whispered as he drew back, retracting what I had taken. Then he rocked into me with one solid trust.

My mouth dropped open with the overload of sensation. It was something I would never get used to, the way Christian felt when he filled me. As if I were complete. Whole. And entirely desperate at the same time, because I would always want more.

"Shit," he whispered, the word thick, heavy as he held himself in check. Still, a satisfied smile spread across that gorgeous mouth. "That is never going to get old."

Agreement rumbled as a hoarse groan at the base of my throat.

No, there wasn't a chance. Christian's touch would forever be familiar, but never, ever would it be routine.

Christian pulled back and filled me again,

decisive and firm, though still conscious of the child, a deliberate caution with each roll of his hips. This man...no...there was no question that he was my all. He spun me up and turned me inside out. Made me feel as if I was walking off a ledge in the same second I felt most protected within the safety of his hold. I wrapped my arms around him, buried my face in his chest as he worked and strained over me, and I completely let go. The blanket covered us, Christian's body dancing with mine as the soft glow of the fire crawled up the walls, wrapping us tight.

Comfort surged, spun with the knot steadily building in my core.

Even though I could tell he was trying to hold them in, harsh grunts kept rising and escaping his mouth. His heart thundered and matched with the frantic beat of mine. Christian pulled back and stared down at me, his blue eyes shining with eternity.

Then he smiled that smile that was only meant for me.

We were one.

There was no greater joy than this. No greater joy than being in his arms. The life I'd spent so many years longing for had been found in the devotion of this man. A connection that could never be severed, even in all those lonely, isolated years we'd spent apart.

"You are my life," he murmured, his eyes unwavering as they watched down on me. He grabbed my left arm that was wrapped around his neck, brought it between us as he tenderly kissed the ring that I wore proudly on my finger.

I stared up at the man who possessed my heart, the one who owned my spirit, and whispered, "And I'm going to give you mine."

seven

*A*wareness surged into my consciousness. I fought to hold onto the darkness, to press my eyes shut so I could remain in the sanctuary of sleep. Reluctantly my eyes fluttered open in the dense fabric of the pillow I had my face buried in. A groggy haze clouded my senses, and my mind reeled as I struggled to make sense of what it was that had jarred me awake.

Lying on my stomach, I lifted my head. I blinked as my sight slowly adjusted to the muted light bleeding in from the heavy drapes I had pulled over the window. I squinted in the direction of my door. Knocking continued to resonate from downstairs. I rammed my face back into the refuge of the pillow, willing whoever was pounding at my front door to disappear.

I should have known that would never be my luck.

A key rattled in the lock. The front door unlatched and it slowly whined open.

My pulse stuttered. Not in fear, but because I didn't think I could handle this today.

Every time, it was the same.

"Liz?" traveled up the stairs on a direct pathway to my unwilling ears.

Natalie.

I didn't respond. Instead I gripped the pillow, forcing my face deep into the fabric. Maybe if I bored into it hard enough, it would swallow me whole. Maybe…maybe I could just disappear.

Footsteps creaked on the stairs. "Liz?" she called again, quieter this time. I squeezed my eyes tighter when I felt her presence emerge. My bedroom door sitting half ajar slowly swung open all the way.

Tension hovered as a thick silence between us before, "Elizabeth," finally flooded into my room on a troubled breath.

Gathering the energy, I forced myself to turn toward her. I rested my cheek on the pillow, blinking over at my cousin who stood in my doorway with worry etching every line on her young face.

She'd grown her hair out a bit, the dark blonde locks curling in a soft wave just over her shoulders. She wore her normal—a thin, over-sized sweatshirt with the neck cut out so it hung loosely off one shoulder, short-short cutoffs, and flip-flops. She turned up a soft smile.

Casual and kind. She always was.

"Hey," she said quietly as she chanced a step into my room.

"Hey," I returned, my voice scratchy against my dry throat. I tried to pretend as if I was happy to see her. And it wasn't like I didn't want to see her, that I didn't care about her or want her to be here. It was just the way she looked at me, as if she could possibly understand. Sympathy I didn't want oozed from her pores. Her movements were slow as she came to stand at the edge of my bed, like maybe if she touched me, I would break.

She seemed unwilling to accept that I was already broken.

"It's time to get up, sweetheart," she almost cooed as she reached out and brushed the hair from my forehead. "I'm here to pick you up. We're going to go to lunch with your mom and your sisters."

Internally I cringed. I knew it wasn't their

intention, but these interventions always felt more like an ambush.

"You should have called first. I don't think I'm feeling up to it today."

Though she tried to hide it, frustration leaked from her sigh. "Come on, Elizabeth. You're never up for it. And you and I both know if I'd have called, you just wouldn't have answered. You need to get out of this house. It's just an hour or two." She strode across my room and raked the drapes back from the window.

Bright light burned into the room. I blanched at the unwelcomed intrusion.

She headed back to the entryway. "Now go jump in the shower. I'll be waiting for you downstairs."

"Nat..." I mumbled, just wishing she would leave me alone.

She crossed her arms over her chest. "We're going to lunch, Elizabeth. You need to eat and your family needs to see you. Two birds with one stone and all." She kind of laughed, though there was little humor to it. It sounded more like disappointment.

I rolled onto my back and draped my arm over my eyes. "What time is it?"

"Just after eleven...which means it's time to get up. Now scoot."

Resigned, I sat up on the side of the bed with

my back to Natalie. I willed myself to leave the place that was my only reprieve. The only remedy for the bleakness of this life was found in the obscured blackness of sleep. Not in the pills they promised would make me feel better but instead just intensified the aching numbness. Not in the counseling sessions that did nothing but stir up the pain, those anguished hours that only amplified the loss.

All I wanted was to sleep.

I didn't dream. I didn't see. I didn't hurt.

I didn't exist.

Get up, I screamed at myself from within my mind.

Sucking in a breath, my feet hit the floor and I pushed myself to stand. Pain rocketed through my body. Something physical. Something real.

Clenching my hands into fists at my sides, I swallowed down the tears that worked their way to my eyes, hoping Natalie wasn't there reading my posture from behind.

"Go on," she prodded at my back.

I forced myself to nod and plodded into my bathroom. I turned the shower as hot as it would go and let it warm up as I shed the clothes I'd worn for days. Grimacing, I stepped into the steaming shower.

Blistering heat scorched me as the water pelted my skin. I made myself stay under it, wishing it could somehow burn this sorrow away, begged for it to cleanse my spirit the same way it did my body.

But it was no use. Unrelenting anguish built up in my chest and burst from my mouth and eyes. Beneath the shower, I placed my hands on the wall and dropped my head, bending at the middle as I gasped for breath. For countless minutes, I gave into it and let myself cry, let my grief go unseen in the water that pounded on my head and back. It streaked in rivulets down my body then dripped onto the tiles of the shower floor before it disappeared down the drain.

Gone.

I clutched my stomach as I wept.

Gone.

And I knew this hurt would never fade.

Swallowing around the emotion lumped in my throat, I forced it all back inside, searching for the numbness. The last thing I needed was for Natalie to think she needed to come up here to check on me. Quickly I washed, then turned off the shower.

I dried and dressed. Mindlessly I ran a brush through the long length of my hair.

I didn't dare look in the mirror.

Inhaling, I searched inside myself for some semblance of normalcy, and I trained my expression as I left my room and started down the stairs. I gripped at the railing as I took them one by one.

Natalie looked up from where she stood in front of the couch, facing the stairs as she folded laundry.

"You don't need to do that," I fumbled through the embarrassment that surged through me.

"Pssh." She smiled a smile that was much too fake. "I don't mind laundry at all." She inclined her head to the towering pile. "Besides, it looks like you could use some help."

I knew she meant it to be nice, but it punched me in the chest. I'd become helpless. Worthless. I couldn't even fold my daughter's laundry. It was pathetic.

What was hardest for me was the fact that Christian was still financially taking care of me. Every two weeks, he deposited money into the account we shared, one we'd opened together as we'd started out on what was supposed to be our life together. A life I now had to accept was never meant to be. He never touched any of it, either, and I knew he left that money for me.

It was humiliating. Demeaning.

Yet I took it because I didn't know what else to do. The thought of having to get up every day and go to work churned my gut into a frenzy of anxiety. So I took from the man I had broken, or maybe he had broken me.

My chest squeezed.

The truth was, it was life that had broken us

both, ripping from us what we didn't know how to live without.

Natalie folded one of Lizzie's shirts and stacked it on top of the growing pile. "So how are you feeling today?" she said in the most casual way, but with the heaviest of undertones.

God.

Every time I saw my family, it was the same—them looking at me, waiting for me to snap out of it, all of them constantly telling me one day it would be okay. Resentment had steadily built, because none of them understood. I'd gotten to the point where I didn't even want to see them, didn't want to be in their presence, because all they did was encourage and judge and prod and promise me things that could never be. None of them knew what they were talking about.

They didn't.

They couldn't.

I stood at the bottom of the last step, clinging to the railing as if it were a lifeline. "I'm actually feeling pretty well today. You know what, why don't you go on without me? While I have the energy, I think I'd better clean up some stuff around here. The house could really use a good cleaning."

Frowning, she lifted a brow as she called my bluff. "You can clean later. And we have reservations. Come on, let's go." She tossed the last shirt on the folded pile and grabbed her purse from the floor.

She headed out the door, leaving it wide open behind her.

Sighing, I followed, knowing there was no chance I was going to get out of this. I stepped outside into the day. Natalie already sat waiting for me in her little, white four-door sedan.

In surrender, I settled into the front passenger seat.

The ten-minute drive to the restaurant was taken in near silence. Natalie continually stole glances at me, kneading the steering wheel as if she were building up the nerve to say something. I kept my attention trained on my fingers that I twisted on my lap, just wishing for the next hour to be over with.

Natalie pulled into the restaurant parking lot, found a spot, and cut the engine. I stepped from the car. My attention darted around to see the parked cars of the women of my family who'd gathered. The ones who were always there to support and love.

A wave of guilt crashed over me.

God, what was wrong with me?

These women only cared about me.

I dropped my head, squeezing my eyes shut as I put a hand out to steady myself on the car, knowing I'd do anything to make it back, to dig myself out of this hole that I had fallen into.

I just didn't know the way.

"Are you ready, sweetie?" Natalie asked as she climbed from her car. Brown eyes full of worry met mine over the roof of the car.

"Yeah," I lied.

She smiled and inclined her head toward the restaurant door. "Come on, I'm starving. Let's get something to eat."

I followed her inside. Small, square tables filled the entirety of the authentic Mexican restaurant. A din of voices rose up in the intimate space as waitresses rushed around during the busy lunch hour, casting quick smiles as they wove through the tables to serve their guests.

Toward the back of the restaurant, where two tables had been pushed together to accommodate all of us, Sarah waved wildly above her head.

"There they are!" Natalie lifted her own hand and waved. She grabbed one of mine and wove us through the crush of tables. "Hey, guys," she said as we approached.

Both of my sisters tossed their napkins to the table as they stood, greetings on their smiling faces.

"You made it," Sarah, my older sister, said as she rounded the table and pulled me into her arms. Her hold was warm in its unending support.

I stiffened.

I knew she noticed my reaction, and still, she

only hugged me tighter.

"It's so good to see you, Elizabeth," she murmured quietly, pulling back to look me in the face.

"It's good to see you, too," I said. I knew somewhere inside me it was the truth.

Squeezing me by the upper arms, she stepped back.

Carrie, my younger sister, was hugging Natalie before she pranced over to me. A cheery smile split her face. "Elizabeth! God, where have you been? I miss you." She hugged me a little too hard.

I struggled to breathe.

It was always a chore, forcing the air in and out of my lungs, taking in this requirement for life. It was a hundredfold in the presence of her overzealous welcome.

And it wasn't her fault, I knew. That was just it. Of everyone here, Carrie was the one who understood the least. She'd spoken words that had cut through me with the force of a knife.

It just wasn't meant to be.

I knew she truly only meant it as encouragement.

Still, it'd made me want to rip her face off, to scream at her and tell her to shut her mouth.

Instead I'd ended up on my knees, puking, trying to purge her comment from my consciousness.

"Miss you, too," I forced myself to say, like with my older sister, knowing somewhere inside me I felt it, even if it was obscured.

She bounced back and plopped back down into her seat.

Slowly Mom rose from her chair. Her approach was calculated as she watched me. I'd been avoiding her. I didn't know why. I just couldn't handle the way she looked at me. I understood how hard it was for her to see me this way, that I too only wanted joy for my own child. It would kill me if Lizzie had to go through something like this in her life. It made me want to wrap her up and shut her away, keep her protected from any tragedy that could befall her.

Maybe I was broken. But there were enough pieces left of me that I still adored my daughter.

That's the one thing in this messed up life I was giving thanks for. Lizzie my light, Lizzie my life.

She was the hope that coaxed me out of bed in the morning, what gave me the ability to put one foot in front of the other, the last bit of drive that sustained my weary soul.

Through all of this, I was able to recognize that my mom felt the same for me.

Strong arms wrapped me up, my arms pinned between us, Mom's rough voice low. "Thank you for coming." She tilted her head to the side as she studied me, every movement meaningful, full of support.

I nodded and lied. "I wouldn't have missed it."

She pursed her lips and dipped her head once, accepting the deception for what it was.

I took my seat and opened the menu in front of me.

Conversation struck up at the table, the four of them chatting about their days. The inconsequentials of their lives rose to the surface of their chatter, but it was obviously there to cover up the undercurrent of strain stretching us all tight. Uneasy eyes darted and searched, peeking at me from over their menus and casting furtive glances they probably didn't think I noticed.

I shifted in discomfort.

Why had I let Natalie talk me into this?

Thankfully the waitress came and rescued me from the scrutiny that had taken hold of the table.

She left and returned quickly with my iced tea. "Your food should be out shortly. Let me know if there's anything I can get you in the meantime," she said as she placed the drink down in front of me.

I mumbled, "Thank you," turned back to the table, and let my gaze drift over the women who had always stood by my side. They had always been the ones to rally around me, no matter what the circumstances. Once again, I knew they were here to pick me up when I was down.

Little did they know it was an impossible feat.

I did my best to keep up with the words they spoke. I tried to listen to the details about their families, the things that were important to them, near to their hearts. Sarah talked endlessly about her children. Angie had won the spelling bee and Brandon had started a new season of football. She talked of how excited he was that he now got to play tackle, how terrified she was to finally allow him to take part in it.

Carrie had met someone new, someone who must have made an impact on her, because she giggled and her cheeks flushed red with just the mention of his name. My little sister didn't do embarrassed. Yet she went on about this guy for the longest time, filling us in on every aspect of his life and how she was sure it would fit into hers.

I dropped my face and pressed my eyes shut, begging for *it* to return, for me to be able to *feel* it, to be excited for them, too.

I felt like the worst person in the world, because I just couldn't find it in myself to care.

And I wanted to.

God, did any of them really understand how much I wanted to?

They droned on, and their words began to bleed together, spreading out in a thin haze that blurred at the fringes of my mind. Our food was served, and I pushed it around my plate, trying to build up the appetite to take a single bite. Laughter and giggles and sounds of surprise beat against my ears, but didn't penetrate deep enough to touch my distorted sense of awareness.

"Liz," Sarah said, her voice taking on an edge of frustration. "Did you hear anything I just said?"

I jerked up. Blinking, I looked at her from across the table. My mind flicked like a reel back through the conversation that had just transpired, grasping for anything that would give me a clue as to where the topic had strayed.

Displeasure flashed on her face. "Were you even listening?"

"Sarah." Natalie slanted her head in a silent plea, her eyes widening. I swore I thought she kicked her under the table.

Sarah and I had always been close. She'd been the one I'd run to as a girl, the one who always seemed to have this natural wisdom, had insight into things I couldn't see. And she rarely deviated from her straight-lined demeanor.

Sarah's attention shot to Natalie. "What?" she said defensively, as if she couldn't believe Natalie was trying to dissuade her from speaking.

But obviously, that didn't apply for today.

Her eyes darted back to me. They blazed with emotion, sympathy and outrage and disappointment. "You have to pull yourself out of this, Elizabeth."

At her words, I felt all the blood drain from my face. Sickness coiled, soured in my stomach as a swell of nausea swept through me.

It was bad enough when they made little comments, the ones that were meant to bolster when they really felt like a slap to the face.

But this…this didn't just seem like an ambush. It was an ambush, an attack I wasn't prepared for.

One I would never be ready to face.

"You've sat there this entire time and not said one word. Not one word," she emphasized.

"Please, don't do this right now, Sarah," Natalie begged, her voice coming out low. Her attention shifted between us as she bit at her lip. Tears rimmed her eyes.

I knew they were both trying to protect me, each in their own way.

Harshly Sarah shook her head. "We've tiptoed around this for too long, Natalie." Even though she spoke to Natalie, her stare never strayed from my face. "It's been almost four months, Elizabeth. And I promise you I'm only telling you this because I love you, but you have to make a decision. It's time you picked yourself up and started living again. For you. For your daughter. Start paying attention to the rest of your family"— she flung her hand out around the table—"because everything is just passing you by. Even when you're here, you're not present. And we all need you back."

My face pinched as I slowly shook my head, struggling to see through the pain that tore through my entire being. I began to rock, my fingers twisting together in the tightest knot as I tried to deflect what was coming from Sarah's mouth.

My head screamed at me that what she said was the truth, while my heart shrank, willing the rest of me to retreat.

It seemed like once she got started, she couldn't stop, the worry and frustration boiling over.

"And what about Christian? The man who would crawl on his hands and knees through hot coals for you? The one who would gladly die for you? Have you stopped to look at him lately?"

Recoiling at the insinuation, I dropped my face to the side to protect myself from the things I didn't want to hear.

"I'm serious, Elizabeth, have you stopped to really look at him? Because he is just as heartbroken as you. It's time you either find it somewhere inside yourself to love him again or cut him loose. Walk away from him, Elizabeth, put him out of his misery, because the man is hanging by a loose thread. Do you even see what this has done to him? What you're doing to him?"

I cringed, sinking deeper into my chair. Of course I saw it. I bore witness to it each morning when he came to pick up Lizzie. And I had cut him loose, had told him to go, and he had. But there would always be something that tethered us, a connection that neither of us could break.

How was that bond not enough to hold us together?

I forced myself to look at her when all I really wanted to do was hide.

"Sarah," I begged, my voice cracking. Tears built and I tried my best to keep them back, to keep them in. But there was nothing I could do. They were unstoppable as they began to fall. "You don't understand."

"Damn it, Elizabeth," she said as she leaned in close over the table, her voice firm. "I know I don't. I'm not pretending that I do. But whether I understand or not doesn't change the fact that it's *time*."

Her words slashed through me, cutting me to the core.

To my left, Mom gently touched my arm, sadness woven through her expression.

"Your sister is right, Elizabeth. I know you don't want to hear it, but we all love you too much to stand aside and watch you fade away. I'm not willing to sit here and allow this to go on any longer without saying something." She glanced at the bones jutting from my arms, let them wander over my protruding collarbones. "Have you looked in the mirror lately? Have you seen what you've allowed this to do to you?"

Allowed *this* to do to me?

Anger tightened the knots in my stomach.

My mom, of all people, should understand.

I shoved my chair back from the table and jumped up.

"I didn't ask for this," I spat at the table, my gaze discordant as it bounced between the women who sat there staring up at me in shock. "I didn't ask for this to happen and I sure as hell didn't ask for your opinions or your advice." I gripped at my aching chest. "Just leave me alone," I pleaded. "Please, all of you, just leave me alone."

Then I turned and fled the tortured confines of the restaurant, rushing past people who dropped silverware to their plates as they gaped at me. I ran out into the warm afternoon sun. I lifted my face to it, searching for the breath that always seemed just out of reach, as if the capacity of my lungs had been cut in half, fragmented, and I could never fully take in what was needed to live.

Because I was dying.

"Elizabeth," rushed from Natalie in blatant relief as she came running out behind me. She stood there, hesitant as she took me in. Finally, she said, "Come on. Let me take you home."

Distraught, I nodded through my tears and followed her across the lot. She kept her hand on my elbow as she led me to the passenger door. She unlocked it and held it open for me.

We said nothing as she drove the short distance back to my house. She came to a stop at the bottom of the driveway. I could feel the intensity of her gaze burning into the side of my face while I fisted the straps of my purse in my hands, staring down at my knuckles turning white as I did everything I could not to fall apart.

"I'm so sorry, Liz." Her voice was quiet. "Please..." She choked over her own tears. "Please don't think we planned that, because we didn't. Everyone is just worried about you."

I looked over at the regret swimming though her glistening eyes. The two of us just sat there, watching the other cry, not knowing how to make sense of this mess, because neither of us wanted to be a part of it.

She cleared her throat and shook her head. "But what Sarah said, maybe it was wrong the way she did it, I don't know. But what she said was true. It's *time*," she stressed.

Maybe the problem was I didn't know what my life looked like on the other side of this. I'd always believed Christian was at the end, and now, I couldn't see him anywhere. How did I move on from that? From the hopes that had been shattered?

"I don't even remember how to breathe,

Natalie," I admitted softly, dropping my face toward my lap as I clutched my purse straps a little tighter. "How can I go on when I've forgotten how to live?"

Peeking up at her, I saw her chewing on her quivering lip, obviously unsure of how to poise her words. She inclined her head and asked in all seriousness, "Do you still love him?"

A suggestion of Christian ghosted across my skin, memories of my life that meant the most to me, love and joy and everything. Sadness welled up and I swallowed it down.

"I don't know," I whispered.

More tears trailed down her face, maybe in direct empathy to mine. Her attention traveled out the windshield where she stared at the empty street. We sat in the excruciating silence.

"Then maybe you need to remember how to live without him, Elizabeth, because you can't continue on this way." There was no accusation in the statement, just her own pain, her words filled with a sharp sense of surrender.

I felt them deep, because I somehow knew she meant that surrender for me, that it was time I moved on. Even if it was without Christian.

I glanced at the clock. It was only thirty minutes before I was supposed to pick my daughter up from school. Her sweet face flickered in my mind, my devotion to her unending, and I knew, most of all, my daughter needed me.

"I will try," I promised my cousin, my friend, but inside I was reeling because who I really needed to convince was myself.

Over the console, she reached for me, wrapping me up in a fierce embrace before she pulled away and earnestly held my face, her own all splotchy and red.

"You will make it through this," she said. "You know that, don't you?"

I shook my head in her hold. Because I still didn't know if I really would. "I need to go and pick up Lizzie," I mumbled because I'd had all of this conversation that I could handle.

I'd said I would try, and that was all I could give.

She nodded once and I climbed from her car.

eight

From behind, Christian grabbed for me. Needy hands slid over my hips to my front. He anchored both of them across my protruding stomach in the same second he buried his face in my neck.

I leaned back into him, unable to stop the small giggle that flitted from my mouth.

He squeezed me a little, the warmth of him spreading out to touch every fiber of my being. "I'm going to miss you," he grumbled hoarsely near my ear before he burrowed through my hair to kiss my neck, sending a thrill of nerves racing through my body.

I moaned my agreement.

"Would you two knock it off!" Natalie yelled from where she tossed a bunch of bags into her trunk. She was parked on the street at the end of my driveway. "You're worse than two teenagers who have ten minutes to make out before their parents get home." She slammed her trunk shut. "You'll see each other tomorrow."

"I'm not quite ready to let her go yet," Christian mumbled mostly to me.

Natalie propped an annoyed hand on her hip. "We have stuff we have to take care of for the wedding before her shower today."

Christian rocked us in a slow sway, his body flattened against mine, every inch of him plastered to me.

It was unbelievable how much I loved it. How much I loved this. I clasped my hands over his that were splayed wide over my belly and rested against the strength of his chest.

Christian's voice deepened, the words hoarse. "I don't think you have anything to worry about, Natalie. As long as the wedding includes me dancing with my wife and her ending up in my bed afterward, everything is going to be perfect."

A shot of choked laughter ripped from Natalie's throat, and she turned her wide, disbelieving eyes on me. "What did you do to him, Elizabeth? I think you've created a monster."

I just grinned. She had no idea. She'd not known the cocky boy I met in college, that flirty mouth and those impatient hands that had turned me upside down, twisted me inside out. The Christian she'd known had been one filled with regret, every moment spent trying to make up for what he'd done.

Christian pulled me closer, his mouth curled up in a self-satisfied smirk. "What? We have a lot of time to make up for."

Now I could recognize that eager boy swimming through the spirit of this caring man. This was the Christian who'd knocked me from my feet, stolen my breath just as assuredly as he'd stolen my heart.

"Let me love on my future wife before you steal her away," he continued.

Natalie scoffed. "Umm…okay, I'm taking her for her final dress fitting and then to her bridal shower, and Matthew is getting ready to take you off on some crazy boys' night somewhere he wouldn't even tell me. Now tell me who's doing the stealing?"

Matthew laughed as he surprised her from behind, lifting her off her feet.

Natalie squealed, but there was no way she could hide the grin that captured her face.

He placed her on her feet and spun her around in the same second. By her waist, he tugged her close and bent her back as he hovered over her. "You're not worried, are you?" His grin was as big as hers.

She swatted at him. "Of course not, but if these two don't knock it off, they're going to make us late."

He pecked her lips. "Good. Because I'm going to take our Christian here and make sure he has a good time." He raised a cocky brow at Christian. "I don't think this guy has left her bed in months," he said, gesturing at me with his chin.

I giggled more as Christian rocked me from behind, his laughter all brash with Matthew's taunting.

"Well considering that's the only place I want to be..." he said as he tipped his head in overt suggestion.

A rush of color seeped to my cheeks with Christian's blatant innuendo.

Still, it was true. Christian and I couldn't get enough of each other. We never would. The need between us came unending, this powerful force that shot through me every time he touched me.

To top it off, we were excited. All of us. It was a joy that sat like a palpable aura in the warm San Diego air. Like I could reach out and touch it.

One week from today, I would be Christian's wife.

I bit my bottom lip to hide the pleasure that lit

deep within me. Christian hugged me closer, and I knew he felt the power of it, too.

Slowly turning me in his arms, an affectionate smile lifted his mouth as he lightly bumped my stomach with his. Gentle fingertips caressed down my sides until he found his way below the distinct prominence jutting out from my belly.

This was the only evidence of my pregnancy, the massive ball that sat out in front of me like a declaration of my and Christian's love. The rest of my body remained thin, probably too thin, but I wasn't nearly as bad off as I was with Lizzie. I felt healthy. Good. That was all I could ask for. Christian kept telling me he was worried I should be gaining more weight, but my doctor assured us that, as long as the baby grew, we didn't have anything to be concerned about.

Christian turned those strong fingers up and tenderly cradled her. Our baby girl. Lillie. Lizzie had named her because she wanted her little sister to have a name like hers. Christian and I didn't hesitate to agree.

It was perfect.

I stared up at him as he ran his thumbs just under my belly button. "I love her," he whispered, "and I love you." He watched down on me with those kind blue eyes that somehow still managed to burn. Christian's attention found its way back to my ear, his breath hot as it caressed along my skin.

"You know I'd much rather spend tonight in bed with you, don't you?" he murmured.

A shiver traveled the length of my body. "Mmmhmm…I bet you're going to miss me while you're out partying with the guys," I teased, although I knew he wasn't speaking anything but the truth.

He released a warm chuckle at my neck as he brushed my hair back, kissing me there. "You're way more interesting. Believe me."

I smirked a little as I weaved my fingers through black strands of soft hair, lifting my jaw so he could kiss miss me a little more.

Natalie smacked her hands together as if shooing away a wild animal. "That's it. Break it up."

I laughed and stepped back. With widened eyes, I mouthed, "Fine," at her.

She returned the same mocking glare, but I saw it all there, sparkling in her eyes. Relief softly played across her features as she watched us, her expression reflecting joy—her joy for me. I knew she'd worried about me for so long, that she'd hoped and prayed that I would one day find a way to heal the broken heart that had tainted every aspect of my life.

Never could I have imagined that those fractured pieces would be mended in the arms of the one who'd shattered me in the first place.

I'd thought I'd lost the ability to love, the ability to forgive. But forgiveness had come into my life like the most intense burst of light. It had penetrated the darkest recesses of my spirit, the hidden places soiled with bitterness, this poison that had eaten and destroyed everything good in me until only fear remained. I'd been chained, bound by my anger. Ridding my heart of it had changed everything. No, I wasn't a new person.

I'd just found myself again.

An affected smile hinted at my mouth. I gazed across at her, a silent confirmation that told her just how happy I really was.

Behind me, footsteps clamored from the house and down the sidewalk. I turned to find Christian's mom, Claire, standing at the end of the walkway, with Lizzie's hand wrapped in hers. Her face was filled with a joy unlike anything I'd ever seen her wear. She'd come into town just two days before, here to share in the festivities of the upcoming week. She'd stay two weeks after the wedding to help my mom take care of Lizzie while Christian and I were away on our honeymoon.

Affection poured from Christian as his gaze settled on the two of them. "Well, now that I have all my girls here, I really don't think I want to leave."

"Daddy," Lizzie scolded with her toothy grin, dimples denting her cheeks. She'd matured so much over the last year. We celebrated her sixth birthday just last weekend. Sometimes it was unbelievable how fast she'd grown, that my round-faced baby was growing into a little girl.

Still, she remained the sweetest thing I'd ever seen.

"You have a party. You *have* to go," she continued on as she rocked onto the outside of her feet and swayed at her grandmother's side.

My heart swelled a little further.

Was it possible to be happier than I was now?

I looked between the faces of the family I loved, and thought no, not a chance. Christian had given me back everything I had lost, completed me in a way I never thought imaginable.

"You'd better go and give your daddy a hug goodbye before he leaves," Claire prodded as she slanted a knowing smile at her son. I loved seeing Christian and Claire this way. Close, each other's staunchest supporter, defender, and friend.

Two nights ago, when we'd picked her up from the airport, I couldn't stop crying as I clung to her, so grateful for how important this woman had become in my life. How crazy it was that she'd once been someone I despised, one I thought was only there to heap more burden on her son, that she really didn't love him the way a mother should. When in reality, she had one of the greatest hearts of anyone I'd ever known. This was only the second time I'd seen her since Christian and I had reconciled. Still, we spent hours on the phone, talking as if we were the oldest of friends, and then there were the times she was there to offer me motherly advice. So easily she fit into both roles.

Lizzie ran down the drive to Christian, and he scooped her up and spun her around.

"I'm going to miss you, princess. You have a fun time at your friend's house."

After the fitting, we'd be dropping her off at Kelsey's mother's house for the evening. We figured a bridal shower wasn't the best place for a six-year-old impressionable little girl. No doubt, some of these women would be doing their best to embarrass me.

"I will, Daddy," she promised. "I like playing at Kelsey's house, then I get to spend the night at Grammy Linda's house!"

"Well, that works out perfect, then, sweetheart. Be a good girl for me, okay?"

"Daddy…" She squirmed and a roll of giggles escaped her as he tickled her side. "Of course I'll be a good girl."

He softened and kissed her nose. Tenderness filled his expression. "I know you will, baby girl."

I leaned into them, my hand on Lizzie's back while Christian held her in the crook of his arm, his other wrapped around my waist, Lillie pressed between us. This time, no one bothered us as we stood there as one. A family.

The way we were always supposed to be.

Mirrors rose up on every side. Quiet rumblings whispered back from them, stirred something deep inside me, uttering my forgotten hopes and dreams. They murmured of a future I'd longed for as a little girl. One where it was love that conquered all.

So badly I'd wanted that for my life, but years ago, I'd given up on that perfect picture, counted it as loss.

Standing here now, those hopes came rushing back, kindling the remnants of those days of my life that had been filled with such a pure, unassuming innocence. It set those hopes aflame and ignited my dreams anew.

My attention wandered the length of the mirror, taking in the simple strapless gown. It had a bodice of delicately braided white lace and a thick ribbon sash that fit snugly just above my expanding waist. It gave way to a cascade of tulle that fell in soft waves down my body. The dress flowed all the way to the floor, and the material was fuller in the back with just the hint of a train.

A swell of emotion surged, pumped steadily through my veins, joy and peace and ecstasy.

How, in such a short time, had my life gone

from empty to complete? Less than a year ago, I'd spent my nights alone, yielding to the belief that I always would be. Now they were spent in the safety of his arms.

Christian had once again changed the direction of my life, this force of a man that I could never have resisted. I never should have tried.

Because a life with him was the only thing I wanted.

"Oh my God, Elizabeth," Natalie whispered at my side. Her fingertips were pressed to her lips. "It's...perfect."

Through the mirror, Natalie met my watery gaze. I let mine wander to my daughter who bounced beside her.

"You look so pretty, Mommy...like a princess," she asserted through her precious grin.

A tremulous smile edged my mouth as I looked down upon the little girl I loved with all my life. I slanted my hand over the soft material covering my stomach, where this new life blossomed. Somehow this baby girl managed to fill me just as full. Not for a second did she take away from the love I held for Lizzie. She just magnified what was already in my heart.

"And look at you, precious girl. You are going to steal the show," I promised her.

Redness flooded Lizzie's face as she twirled the silken material of her baby blue flower-girl dress.

She giggled. Bashfully, she whispered, "I think I look like a princess, too, Mommy."

From over my shoulder, I caught my mother watching me with outright adoration.

In the beginning, she'd had reservations about Christian and me. It wasn't that she didn't want us to be together, it was just that she believed we were rushing into things too quickly, the way we'd upped the wedding date, definitely when we told her we were expecting. She'd wanted us to give it time so we could find if we really could fit back into each other's lives, for trust and belief to build before we made any permanent commitments.

But time had brought that all to an end, because time could never change what Christian and I shared. A strong relationship had steadily built between Christian and my mother. It was one that was so incredibly important to me because I loved them both more than should have been possible. I couldn't stand for any riffs to remain between them.

The same awe I was feeling shined back at me. Moisture swam in her eyes, glistening in the warm brown. "You're beautiful, Elizabeth. Unbelievably beautiful," she said.

Her words tightened my chest and made it hard to breathe. "Don't make me cry," I demanded, pressing my fingers into the hollow beneath my eyes, trying to rein in the emotion that was vying for release.

But it was already too late.

Tears worked their way free and slipped down my cheeks, a fervent display of everything I'd ever wanted. Frantically I rubbed them away. "Oh my god, I'm going to cry all over my wedding dress."

From where she stood beside my mother, Claire watched me with her own elation shining through. Chewing at her bottom lip, she struggled to control her brimming emotions that quickly overflowed.

And I was trying not to laugh, trying not to cry, knowing that I looked a complete mess, because all of this was entirely overwhelming.

I was going to marry Christian.

The realization hit me hard.

Natalie choked over the tears that welled up in her throat, laughing over the sob she seemed to be struggling to keep in.

The seamstress who'd done my final alterations probably thought all of us insane, these grown women standing in the middle of the bridal dressing room, crying through their laughter.

Natalie wiped her wet cheeks, her smile unending. Then she shook her head with a grin. "Christian is going to lose it when he sees you in that dress."

My gaze traveled back to my reflection. Redness seeped across my chest and flamed at my cheeks, because I couldn't help but picture the expression

Christian would wear when he first caught sight of me. But what struck me most was I could only imagine how it was going to feel when I finally walked down the aisle toward the man who owned me, heart and soul. The one who held me in his hands and captured every thought in my mind.

I couldn't wait to stand before him in this dress and promise him my life.

nine

On Thursday afternoon, I pulled up close to the curb in the circular drive in front of Lizzie's school. I cut the engine to my little red Honda and glanced at the clock glowing from the dash. Only three minutes until the last bell rang. Yearning nudged me somewhere in my chest. It was just a little thump of awareness. But it was there. It was a feeling I hadn't truly experienced in so long. I'd longed and I'd mourned, but I realized then I hadn't really *wanted*.

And I wanted Lizzie.

Two days had passed since I last saw my little girl. She spent Tuesday and Wednesday nights with her dad. Even though I always missed her, there was a grim resignation that always came with it. It was then I'd find myself lost in the oblivion of sleep, wasting away the minutes and hours, letting go of those days of my life because I didn't want to live them.

But today was different. I wasn't sure what it was. This morning I woke early. I'd gotten up and cleaned the house, went out in the backyard and puttered around in the flower bed, had showered and changed.

I even looked in the mirror, studying what my mother had seen earlier in the week, the hollow woman who'd been staring back at me. Almost frantically, I put makeup on, as if I could cover it up, hide what was festering inside of me.

And I knew it was only a temporary solution, a patch that couldn't hold.

Still, I found some sense of satisfaction in it.

Now I was anxious. I gripped the steering wheel, willing time to pass. I couldn't wait to wrap Lizzie in my arms.

After what seemed an eternity, the bell rang. Seconds later, children began to flood through the school gates and out into the open corridor.

I rose from my car and went to stand on the walkway, my attention focused ahead as I strained to catch the first glimpse of my daughter.

"Hey, Liz."

A short gasp escaped me and I jumped when I was hit with the voice that fell much too close to my ear. I pressed my hand to my chest, trying to catch my breath.

"Logan, hi," I wheezed. A disconcerted smile ruffled my mouth as I attempted to regain my composure. Ridiculous, but the man had really startled me.

"I didn't hear you," I said, feeling self-conscious as I peeked up at him from the side.

He laughed, pitching a casual hand through his shaggy, blond hair.

I might have been from California, but Logan definitely owned the look.

"Well, that's because you were about a million miles away." With a grin, he gestured his chin toward the gate. "Or rather, lost within those halls over there."

I smoothed myself out. "Yeah, I guess I was, wasn't I?"

"Are you missing her?" he asked, his expression suddenly serious as he turned his full attention on me.

Taken by surprise at his question, I jerked to look at him. I blinked rapidly as I found him staring down at me. His gaze was intense, like he was searching for an answer inside of me.

I really didn't know him all that well. I'd spoken with him casually when I'd dropped Lizzie off at his house or he'd picked Kelsey up at mine, and we'd shared quick exchanges like this out here in front of the school. But honestly, the last months had passed in such a blur that I really couldn't remember much of our interactions at all, just innocuous hellos and goodbye wishes that meant nothing at all.

Now he was looking at me as if he understood some fundamental piece of me.

He seemed to take my silence as an admission, and he released an empathetic breath. "You know…" He spoke softly, slowly, his hands stuffed deep in the pockets of his shorts. "It's really difficult getting used to at first." He kind of shrugged. "Dropping them off and knowing you won't see them for days. Going home to the obtrusive silence of an empty house." He inclined his head, nodding as if he were convincing me of something I needed to know. "But it does get easier. I can promise you that. Pretty soon, it just becomes a routine. Normal." It almost sounded like defeat.

Is that what this was? Something I would get used to? I chewed at the edge of my bottom lip as I let my attention drift back toward the gates. The idea tumbled around in my head. My first instinct was to reject the notion. No, I just wasn't willing to accept this as normal. But the truth was, I didn't know what normal was anymore.

A shock of black hair that could only belong to Lizzie finally came into view behind the herd of students flocking to their cars. Her ponytail bounced wildly behind her as she skipped along the sidewalk, hand-in-hand with Kelsey. She was smiling, a smile so bright I couldn't help but smile myself.

"Mommy!" she squealed when she caught sight of me. She made a beeline in my direction, Kelsey in tow. "I missed you." She threw her arms around my waist and hugged me. I weaved my arms around her, high up on her back, holding her close to me. God, it felt so good. How much had I missed this child? I realized then, I'd been missing her for much longer than just the last two days.

For a few seconds, she kept her face buried in my stomach before she turned that precious face up to me.

I ran the back of my fingers down the soft skin of her cheek, my head tilted to the side as I looked down at my daughter beaming up at me. "I missed you so much, baby girl. Do you know that?"

Her little hands clung to me, and I felt all of her love. But it was there, too, a trace of her confusion, a hint of her need she kept tucked inside her, hidden away in the same way I hid my own. I sighed in regret as I ran my fingers through the silky strands of her ponytail, a gentle encouragement that somehow, someway, we were going to figure all of this out.

She hugged me a little more before she turned her attention back to Kelsey, who seemed to be permanently attached to her side. "Mommy, when can me and Kelsey play again? We haven't got to play in a whole week," Lizzie said emphatically, the sweet, innocent, little girl making a return.

My voice was soft as I cupped her cheek. "I'm not sure, sweetheart, but I'm sure we can figure something out."

"Kelsey's going to be with me over the weekend." Logan's voice broke into the moment.

I'd almost forgotten he was there. Taking Kelsey's backpack from her, he slung it over one shoulder.

"Why don't you and Lizzie come over Sunday afternoon? We can let the girls play and we can barbecue or something?" He said it in an offhanded way, completely nonchalant.

I hesitated, knowing it should be nothing. Still, it felt like something.

"I don't think that's a good idea right now," I said quietly, turning my gaze down to my feet.

"Oh, please, Mommy, please!" Lizzie begged at my side as she jumped up and down.

Kelsey joined in. "Yes! I wanna have a barbecue!"

I chanced a glance in his direction. Logan grinned at me with his hair flopping down in his face. He flipped it back with a shake of his head.

"It's not a big deal, Liz. Honest…it's just food, and it'll be a ton more fun if we share it with friends."

My deadened senses sparked. Christian fluttered through my consciousness like a breeze, a gust of his presence breathing into me. His touch…a whisper of his mouth. A ripple of need.

An eruption of blinding pain.

I squeezed my eyes to block it all out, this reflex that curled in my stomach and soured in my mouth.

I hated it, hated that I couldn't stop myself from feeling like this whenever I thought of him.

I shook the involuntary reaction away, convincing myself it didn't matter anyway. It wasn't as if this meant anything, because it didn't. It was just something to get me out of the house, something to break me from the cycle I'd given myself over to.

I'd promised Natalie…had promised myself.

I will try.

"Come on, Mommy," Lizzie implored again as she tugged at my hand, looking up at me with hopeful blue eyes.

"Fine." I bit at the inside of my mouth as I agreed, feeling a flicker of unease. "Is there anything I can bring?" I asked warily, giving in and looking up at Logan.

"Nah. Kelsey and I hardly ever get the chance to entertain, so we'd be happy to take care of it all. Right, honey?" he asked as he flashed a mega-watt grin at his beaming daughter.

"Right!" she said with a delighted nod of her head.

"Yay! I get to come over to your house!" Lizzie released my hand and nearly tackled Kelsey, the girls jumping as they squeezed each other in an overt show of excitement.

For the second time today, there was no stopping the smile that prodded at my mouth, the faintest hint of joy manifesting on my face. Seeing my daughter this way, knowing everything she'd been dragged through over the last few months and she still was thriving, brought a feeling of peace over me.

Any discomfort this brought me was worth it.

I will try.

I would try for her.

"So what time do you want us over?" I asked.

"Three sound good?"

"Sure." Unsure would have been a better description of what I was feeling, but I said it anyway. I took Lizzie's hand to start for the car. "We'll see you Sunday, then."

"Oh, and Liz?"

I paused and looked over my shoulder.

Logan's gaze traveled my body before it landed back on my face. "You look really nice today."

Self-consciously, I glanced down at the jeans and tee-shirt I wore, the first real clothes I'd worn to pick Lizzie up in months. I fidgeted with the hem of my shirt as I felt redness bloom on my face. "Uh…yeah…I guess I've looked a mess lately."

His laughter was full of tease, though it rumbled with something more. "Believe me, Liz, no one can rock a pair of scroungy sweats the way you can."

Then he lifted his chin with a smile and turned and led his daughter away.

Ruffled, I stood there watching them go. My mind reeled as I tried to make sense of what had just transpired. I placed an affectionate hand on Lizzie's back. My voice was barely audible over the blaring headache that struck up in my head.

"We better get going."

"Okay, Mommy."

Logan waved back over at me as he climbed into his car.

I will try. For my daughter, I will try.

ten

A roar of catcalls and whistles filled Sarah's small living room. Black lace lay piled in the box I held on my lap, one that had come from Natalie.

"Do they even make lingerie for pregnant girls?" I asked through my grin as my attention sought her out.

She leaned against the wall across the room. Not for a second was I embarrassed. I was enjoying myself too much.

"Um, you weren't supposed to be six-months pregnant on your wedding day, but yes, they most definitely do. I just had to dig a little deeper," Natalie hollered over the din of the raucous room. Playfulness filled up the entirety of her smirk. "And believe me, Christian is going to appreciate my efforts."

I pulled the nightie from the box and held it up in front of me. It had to be the sexiest piece of lingerie, all lace and garters and ribbon...and, well...not much else.

No, I didn't think there'd be any issue with calling Christian's appreciation into question. The only problem would be hiding it from him long enough to save it for our honeymoon. If he found it before, he'd be begging me to wear it.

Discretely I shook my head and bit at my lip. Nothing sounded better than two weeks of just Christian and me, long days and nights spent lost to each other, our hearts, minds, and bodies wrapped up and consumed. Where, he wouldn't tell me, but his eyes had glimmered, a furor of excitement swimming through the depths as he promised me it was somewhere I'd never been before, but he couldn't wait to take me there. It didn't matter where he took me. It'd be paradise simply because we were together.

I folded it up and placed it back in the box. "Well, I'll tell him this is compliments of you." I smirked right back. Then I smiled. "Thank you, Nat. Honestly."

I was thanking her for so much more than simply her gift. She'd put in countless hours planning for this wedding, taking her role as Matron of Honor seriously, almost to the extreme. I was grateful for every second of it. It would never have turned out so perfectly without the work she and my sisters had put into it.

"You're welcome." Sincerity transformed her face.

"Okay, next one," Sarah said. She was perched on the floor at my side, feeding me gifts just as quickly as I could open them.

She set on my lap a small silver gift bag with a beautiful mess of black and silver tissue paper sticking out the top. I fumbled for the card.

Selina.

I slanted her a smile as I pulled out what was nestled inside.

A plain white coffee mug. I rotated it a little, unable to contain my grin as I found the personalization on the front.

Mrs. Davison.

I turned it toward my guests. A round of *oohs* and *aahs* and *that is so sweet* rose up over the room.

I couldn't help but agree.

"I love this. Thank you, Selina."

"You're welcome."

Really I couldn't wait for that to become my name. I was more than ready. The date had become like this beacon, a signal for our future. Even though Christian and I had already begun our lives together, it didn't make the day any less important.

"Here, open mine next." Carrie came forward and grabbed a white gift bag that overflowed with black tissue paper. "Here."

"Well, aren't you in a hurry," I teased as I situated the bag on my lap. "You better not have gotten me something that's going to embarrass me," I warned.

She scoffed. "Don't act like such a prude." She inclined her head toward my stomach that poked out above my fitted jeans. "Because not one of us in this room is going to believe it."

I swatted at her and laughed. "You're terrible."

She just grinned. "Open it," she prodded, anxious.

I closed my eyes and reached into the bag, expecting the worst. If anyone in this room would leave me blushing, it was Carrie.

My fingers grazed across something firm and covered in smooth fabric.

Frowning in question, I opened my eyes and pulled out her gift.

I blinked up at my little sister. She'd always been prone to selfishness, the youngest child, the center of attention. That didn't mean I didn't love her with every ounce of my being. But this...this was kind and thoughtful.

I ran my fingers over the handmade album before I flipped it open to the first page. Pictures were glued to the decorative paper, faded and worn, the colors bleeding away from the youngest days of our youth. My sisters and I were in our mother's backyard. The three of us were in nothing but our underwear, covered in mud, wearing the biggest smiles you'd ever seen three children boast. In another, Christmas had come, and my sisters and I were dressed in footed pajamas, our excitement palpable as we hung our stockings on the mantel. A third was from Easter, frilly pink dresses, a mess of fake, green grass, eggs brimming over the top of our baskets.

The last was our beach.

Tears welled.

I couldn't stop them.

Through glistening eyes, I looked up at my little sister. "This is…perfect."

I turned the pages through the years of our lives, school pictures, plays, soccer games, and sleepovers. We grew and haircuts and styles changed, a progression of time shared, but through all of them was a projection of our joy.

Toward the back, I stood in the football field after receiving my high school diploma, flanked by my mother and my sisters. Our arms were wrapped around each other as we all leaned toward the camera, the four of us grinning like we were preparing to have the greatest tomorrow.

And on the last page of the album, I'd grown. The lines of my face hinted at the woman I would become, though I still wore the innocence of a girl. The picture had been snapped just before I boarded a plane for the first time in my life. I could almost see the wonder that had filled my eyes, the fear and the anxiety all mixed up with the greatest kind of anticipation as I'd set off for New York City.

I could almost feel it now, exactly the way I'd felt then. I knew my life was about to change. I just never imagined how much.

Just days after this picture was taken, I met Christian.

On instinct, my hand sought out my stomach where Lillie kicked me, her little foot jutting out at my side.

Today I felt the same.

My life was about to change.

"Thank you. I can't tell you how much this means to me."

Carrie leaned down and hugged me in a way she never had before. "I just wanted you to see yourself through my eyes...the way I see you. These are my memories of my big sister who I looked up to my entire life. I'll never stop," she promised.

The tears I'd been trying to hold in fell. Sniffling, I wiped them with the back of my hand. "Love you."

Quietly, she spoke. "Love you, too."

"Okay, next one," Sarah piped in, breaking up the heaviness, all smiles as she searched the pile of gifts.

She set a beautifully wrapped package on my lap, silver paper with black and white ribbon. I opened the card. I read the words written in delicate script inside.

My Dearest Elizabeth,

I find myself at a loss to express my joy, my gratitude, and my love for you. They are bountiful. Profuse. Unending.

The only thing a mother ever wants is for her children to be happy. There are so many ways I believe I failed my son, mistakes I made that I can never take back. But I look at him now and see the way he loves you and Lizzie, the way he loves this new baby, and I know I had to have done something right.

And it's you, Elizabeth, you who brings this light out in him, you who makes him shine.

For this, I will be forever grateful.

Never have I told anyone this, but for all of my life, I longed for a little girl to call my own. Christian may have been the only child I bore, but you are my daughter.

I love you, and I wish you and Christian a lifetime of happiness. Be good to each other and never forget what is

important in this world.
Yours,

Claire

My heart clenched. Shakily, my eyes found her across the small room, where she just sat there, watching me as if she'd been projecting each word of that letter to me.

Soundlessly we spoke, a thousand words voiced in silence. Claire was one of my lessons in life, a testament that people may not always be who they seem, and sometimes the purest hearts are buried beneath their own mistakes.

I loved her more for seeing her way through it. Loved her most for seeing through all of mine.

Dragging my attention away, I unwrapped her gift and slowly lifted the lid. Inside, the gift was wrapped in white, shimmery tissue paper, and a tiny note scrawled in script was laid on top.

For your wedding night.

The tissue paper rustled as I pulled it free.

Maybe I was a little surprised. Maybe I really wasn't at all. And it wasn't awkward or weird. I knew she was giving it as her blessing.

Gently I lifted it by the delicate ribbon straps. The nightie was entirely white. Baby-doll style, the soft material looked as if it would brush just along the top of my thighs. The bra and trim were edged in satin, and the rest flowed free in a silky-sheer mesh. It was elegant and altogether sexy.

In awe, I looked up at her. "This is beautiful, Claire."

I was just about as excited to stand in front of Christian wearing this as I was my wedding my dress. No, being with Christian was nothing new. How many times had I made love to him when we were young, when we were all hands and need and desire? As he'd taught me and I'd willingly learned, as I'd begged and he'd pleased. And God, these last months since we'd reunited... I tingled with the thought.

We knew each other's bodies well.

But on our wedding night would be a first, a start and a finish. A culmination. A completion.

"Thank you so much," I whispered.

Prodding, she gestured with her chin. "There's one more there from me."

Sarah was quick to place the second gift on my lap. Smiling, I tugged at the paper and opened it.

My breath caught.

"Now, I know this is your bridal shower, and maybe I should have waited for your baby shower, but I really couldn't resist." An expectant smile flickered across her face, one only a grandmother could wear.

A tiny blanket lay nestled in the box. White with little specks of yellow and green, soft and used and just all around perfect.

She almost hesitated, then rushed out, "That was Christian's. I...I wish that Lizzie would have had the chance to use it. When I kept it, that had been my intention—that it would be handed down to my son's first child. And she should have had it...I wish she would have...but I want this baby to have the chance to represent the beginning of your family."

My fingers traced along the soft material and caressed over a faded stain that hinted at one satiny corner. "This is...amazing, Claire." Tears surfaced again. Fighting them was futile. I wiped at them as they fell. "So I'm going to blame this baby for all these tears I keep crying," I said through soggy laughter.

Claire wiped away her own.

I loved Christian. So much. I always had. It was impossible to love him more, and there was no chance I could love him less.

But sharing this pregnancy with him, gaining back what I'd lost, what I'd so desperately missed, had filled the void that had haunted me for so many years. How intensely had I longed for a family? Only because I'd longed for him. Going through this together, I felt closer to him than I ever had.

I knew he'd appreciate this gift as much as I did.

"Okay, that was the last one," Sarah said as she

began picking up the few stray pieces of tissue paper that had made their way to the floor. She stuffed them inside an empty bag.

Lillie kicked me again. Caught off guard, I jumped with the twinge of pain that bit at me just below my rib. I covered the spot with my hand.

"Is that little girl giving you fits again?" Mom asked. The quiet but firm gentleness that always surrounded her glimmered in her eyes.

"Yes." The fullest smile lifted my mouth as I pressed my hand a little firmer to my side, feeling a slow roll of her movements across my abdomen.

"Can I feel?" Sarah asked. She didn't wait for an answer, because she already knew what it would be, and she reached out to cover my hand with hers.

She tilted her head as if she were studying before awe filled her face. "Oh my God." She glanced up at me with a smile to match my own before she dropped her attention back to where she had her hand plastered across my stomach. "She's moving all over the place. You'd think after having two kids of my own, this wouldn't seem like the coolest thing in the world."

I knew what she meant. Even after having Lizzie, every time this baby moved, I was struck, unable to process how truly amazing it was.

I turned back to my guests. "Thank you all so much...for everything," I said, getting up to embrace each of them. They'd truly showered me with their love and their blessings. Sarah and Natalie placed all the bags near the door, a wealth of candles and perfumes and gift cards that promised me relaxing days at the spa.

My spirit danced in the midst of these women who'd rallied around me. Only this time, it wasn't to pick me up when I was down, but to support me in my time of happiness.

Most stayed for a while as casual conversations struck up in my sister's cozy living room. Eventually people began to leave. Goodbyes were said, hugs, gentle hands pressed to my belly.

I couldn't believe the next time I saw my friends and extended family, it'd be as I began the march down the aisle to marry the man I'd loved for as long as I could remember. The upcoming week would be nonstop, dinners to entertain our guests arriving from out of town, our rehearsal and dinner, and I knew Natalie would be dragging me everywhere as we took care of all the last minute details.

I closed the door with a final wave. The only ones who remained were my sisters, Natalie, my mom, and Claire.

I blew out a heavy breath, realizing just how exhausted I was after today. Everyone headed into the kitchen to begin cleaning up, all except for my mom, who hung out on the other side of the couch, watching me.

"This was a great day, Elizabeth," she said with a subtle nod of her head.

"Amazing. These women…" I looked back at the door they all had just disappeared through. "I can't imagine feeling more loved than I do right now."

She offered me a smile as she pulled a small gift from behind her back. She began to walk toward me. "I have something for you, but I didn't want to give it to you in front of everyone."

A smile wobbled at one corner of my mouth, and I looked at my mom who appeared a little self-conscious, shifting her feet, ill at ease.

The gift was haphazardly wrapped, all over the place with kinks and uneven edges and subdued beauty, a little like my mother's constant demeanor.

Awe pumped a steady beat with my heart, wound with expectancy and hope. Somehow I knew whatever waited inside, her gift was going to become one of my most cherished possessions.

Slowly I extended my hand out between us, palm up, and watched as she carefully sat the gift upon it.

"Thank you," I murmured as I glanced up at her with a soft smile, then down to tug gently at the satin ribbon.

Cautiously, I unwrapped her offering. Tearing

away the tacks of tape, I pulled the paper free. I lifted the lid to the small box.

"Mom," I whispered. Nested inside the white satin lining was a ring.

But not just any ring.

My grandmother's ring.

An old yearning slammed me. It hurt and comforted and filled me whole. I missed my grandma so much, and to be given this was beyond anything I'd ever have expected.

The white gold band appeared the antique it was, worn, though it still boasted the intricate design that wrapped and curled. Delicate tendrils crawled up to cradle a baby blue stone. Pinching it between my fingers, I spun it through the rays of late afternoon light that streaked in through the window, let the colors shimmer and dance and play.

Something old and something blue.

"She gave that to me a few days before she passed," Mom said. A distinct current of homesickness slipped into her tone. "She told me it belonged to you, and that I'd know exactly when I was supposed to give it to you."

Wistful emotion played where it danced along the lines set deep in her face, her mouth quivering. "I know that day's today, Elizabeth. That ring was meant for you to wear on your wedding day."

She swallowed hard. "I have to be honest and

tell you I've been worried over all this for you. When Christian came back into your life, I was scared for you, I guess because of all of my own insecurities…the things I had to go through in my own life." She kind of laughed, though it was drenched in sadness. "For so long, I viewed the two of us the same, and somewhere inside me, I thought we'd live out our days the same way…alone. Like we had this common bond we both had to bear." Her voice strengthened. "What I never imagined was Christian would turn out to be the man he is. But there is no mistaking it in him. I'm so thankful you've found a man to love you the way you deserve to be. Completely."

"Mom," bled from my mouth in a torrent of thankfulness. I rushed to pull her into an eager embrace. "I can't tell you what this means to me. This ring…you saying this. Thank you…so much. You don't even know."

She hugged me tight, her arms wrapped around me in an unwavering declaration of support. "Yes, I do," she whispered back. "I just want you to be happy."

I edged back an inch, still clinging to her, clinging to the ring I had pinched between my fingers. God, I was crying again, but I felt so full. So loved. How could I stop them? Today…well, really, these past few months, had been perfectly overwhelming. Flawlessly breathtaking.

"I don't think I've ever been so happy."

She touched my cheek. "I can see it. You radiate it. Don't ever let it go."

That promise was easy to make. "I won't."

eleven

On Monday night, I turned the key on my condo lock. I held the door open and flipped on the light. "Go on in, sweetheart."

With a passing grin, Lizzie scampered around me into the living area.

I had her pink overnight bag slung over my shoulder, and I dropped it to the floor beside the door.

A wistful smile played at my mouth as I watched my daughter enter my condo. God, I'd been missing her. The last time I'd spent any time with her was Saturday morning before I dropped her back home, and she'd spent the last two nights with Elizabeth. I'd had an early meeting this morning, so I had to ask Elizabeth to take her to school and then she picked her up this afternoon. I'd been anxious all day, wishing the hours away so I could head to Elizabeth's to pick Lizzie up to spend the night with me.

There'd been something I couldn't quite read about Elizabeth this evening.

Maybe I was grasping, but I thought I sensed a change, something I couldn't quite pinpoint. Like maybe there was a subtle difference in her eyes. Like maybe there was a flicker of life. It'd been missing for so long, I almost didn't recognize it, but she'd dropped her gaze faster than I had time to study her, to understand her.

I shook my head. I just didn't know, didn't know what she wanted, didn't know what I could do.

But I knew I was going to have to do something. How much longer would I just sit idle? Doing nothing? An overbearing feeling of helplessness had held me back, kept me down. But I felt it all coming to a head.

I quietly latched the door behind us.

Rays of sunlight streamed in from the floor-to-ceiling windows in my loft. Burning streaks of oranges flamed against the fading blue on the horizon, glimmered across the rippling bay as daylight slipped away.

Lizzie went right for the windows, her favorite spot at my place. "Look at all the sailboats," she whispered, almost pensive as she pressed her face and hands to the glass. "I wish I got to see the ocean every day."

I crept up to her side and rested my hand on the back of her head. "It's really beautiful out there, isn't it?" I cast her a soft smile.

She returned one that eclipsed anything happening outside. "The ocean is my favorite, Daddy."

"I know, princess. I know." It'd become my favorite, too. Something so special to Elizabeth and Lizzie had inevitably become my own. We'd been looking at houses near our beach when everything fell apart. Lizzie had been thrilled, running through each house with unadulterated wonder as she proclaimed almost every single house we looked at as *the one*. I could only pray one day we would finally make it there.

I nudged her chin. "Are you hungry?"

"Uh-huh." She dropped one earnest nod, and a sudden cheerfulness took over her expression. "I'm super hungry, Daddy." She scooted away from the window and into the kitchen. She opened the refrigerator door and peered inside.

Making dinner had become one of her favorite

chores. She always wanted to help plan and cook. These cherished moments we spent in the quiet ease of my kitchen had become one of the things I most looked forward to.

"What should we make?" she asked, a flurry of excitement flooding her voice from where it echoed back from the refrigerator. She had her head buried inside, searching through the stock of food I had ready for her.

"I went to the grocery store yesterday to make sure I had plenty of food for you. I picked up some chicken. I thought maybe we make some mashed potatoes and vegetables with it? How's that sound?"

"That sounds yummy...but I did just have chicken yesterday."

Wandering in behind her, I kind of laughed as I ruffled a playful hand through her hair while I passed by her. As if she wouldn't eat chicken every day. I moved to the opposite side of the kitchen and leaned down to pull a large pot from the lower cupboard and set it on the stove.

"You did, huh? Did your help your mommy make dinner last night?"

"Nope! Me and Mommy had a barbecue at Kelsey's house, and we had barbecue sauce on it, and I ate two whole pieces."

Normally I would have chuckled at my daughter's rambling. Not today.

I stilled as a slow sense of foreboding took hold, a shock of ice-cold awareness penetrating deep as it slithered down my spine. It spread out to freeze every cell in my body. With my eyes narrowed, I turned to look back in her direction. Lizzie was leaning over with her back to me, digging through the vegetables in the bottom crisper.

"You went to a barbecue at Kelsey's house? With Mommy?" I clarified. The words came harsh, forced, because I was sure I wasn't going to be able to stomach her answer.

Lizzie stood and, with her foot, she nudged the refrigerator door closed. Her entire face glowed as she spun around and danced her way over to me with a plastic bag stuffed with broccoli swinging from her hand.

"Oh, Daddy, we had so much fun. Mommy and I spent almost all day there. I got to play for so long, and I got to help put the sauce on the chicken. I was careful not to burn myself, just like you taught me."

On its own accord, my head slowly began to shake, and I felt as if I was being led into a massacre, set up for the kill.

This was not happening. I *refused* to let this happen.

"Here you go," Lizzie prodded at my side, looking up at me in confusion as she handed me the bag of broccoli, completely unaware that her words had cut me to the core.

For once, the child seemed oblivious to the turmoil she'd spun up in me.

"At whose house, Lizzie?" I asked.

Lizzie gave me a look that told me I was crazy. "I already told you, silly. At Kelsey's house."

"Which one of Kelsey's houses?" My voice came out harsher than I intended it to.

Because I already knew.

Shit.

Distraught, I scrubbed my palm over my mouth and dragged it down my chin. It took everything I had not to shout, took everything inside me not to demand Lizzie give me a different answer than the one I already knew she was going to give. This had nothing to do with her, the unwitting messenger who stood there grinning up at me. No chance in hell would I take this out on her. No chance would I show her that the day she was going on and on about was enough to shred what was left of me.

"Oh…" She giggled as if my meaning had just dawned on her. "At her daddy's house."

That asshole. I *knew* it. I fucking knew it.

I forced myself to stand still, because my control was slipping fast. Steadying myself, I pressed my palms onto the counter. The cool surface shocked into my heated hands. Anger pounded through my system, a raging storm that thundered through my veins, an onslaught of fear and outrage and the brutal sense of disappointment that tightly fisted my chest.

Dropping my head, I sucked in a breath and tried to swallow it down. It just lodged at the base of my throat.

I didn't know if I was angrier with myself or with Elizabeth.

What I did know was I wasn't going to let that asshole anywhere near her. Who the fuck did he think he was? Taking advantage of Elizabeth when she was at her most vulnerable?

This wasn't a fucking game.

This was my *family*.

I raked a shaky hand through my hair, then forced a fraudulent smile. The act was physically painful. "Why don't you finish rinsing the broccoli and I'll be right back to help you get it started, okay?"

"Okay, Daddy."

I squeezed my eyes shut, trying to block the images from invading my mind. I searched for my bearings before I started down the hall to my bedroom. Darkness swallowed me as I quietly clicked the door shut behind me. For a second, I stood there, just forcing the stagnant air in and out of my lungs, then I staggered the rest of the way into my bathroom. Blindly I fumbled for the light switch. Light flooded the space, and I blinked to orient myself. Not to the harsh glare shining from the lights above the mirror, but to the cruel reality that I might actually lose her.

I guess somewhere inside me, I'd held onto the belief that one day Elizabeth would open her eyes and really see me. That she'd see me the same way I saw her.

As the one she couldn't live without.

Shit.

How could I have allowed this to happen?

I held myself up on the counter and dropped my head.

Realization crushed me.

Like Matthew had accused me of the other night, I was a fool.

The worst kind of fool.

After everything we'd been through together, I'd left Elizabeth when she needed me most. Left when life was the most difficult, because I didn't know how to deal with the pain any more than she did. We'd been blindsided, our foundation ripped from beneath us, nothing there to catch us when we fell.

And when we'd fallen, we had completely fallen apart.

I'd been standing on the sidelines, waiting. Waiting when I should have been fighting.

I lifted my face to find my reflection staring back at me. My eyes swam with torment, swamped in a grief that felt unending and echoed the loneliness that was eating me from the inside out. It was destroying the last piece of me, my last bit of hope that somehow we'd make it out of this together.

But what was Elizabeth supposed to think when she woke without me morning after morning? What was she supposed to feel? Was she supposed to believe I loved her, that I'd stand by her side no matter what came our way, like I'd promised her I would?

Fuck.

I squeezed my hands into fists.

What had I done?

I felt a glimmer of Elizabeth's touch, felt her mouth near my ear as she promised, *I'm going to love you forever.*

My chest tightened and my head spun.

The truth was, even though it was Elizabeth who'd forced me out, I'd walked away because it was too *hard*. Because life was hard and unfair. Because Elizabeth was hurting and she hurt me in return. Because I couldn't stand to stay there and watch her suffer anymore. I realized now that seeing her that way had cut me so deeply, I didn't know how to handle it.

I'd had the overpowering urge to shake her, to force her to snap out of it, because all I wanted was to see her smile again. I should have just sat by her side, taken it, *endured it*, even when the distance between us had seemed insurmountable.

I should have *stayed*.

I always knew, even though she never came straight out and said it, somewhere inside of Elizabeth, she believed I had let her down.

I had to admit now that I had.

I'd been so wrapped up in giving her perfection, I hadn't been prepared to hold her up when devastation hit.

twelve

The incessant call of the alarm clock beeped from my nightstand. With almost a smile, I quickly reached out and silenced it. I was already awake. I lay on my back, staring at the shadows that rose then faded on the ceiling. Early morning threatened at the window. To my right, Elizabeth's deep, even breaths bled into the silence, like a harmony that played at my ear.

The deepest sense of contentment blanketed me.

I rolled onto my side, careful not to wake her.

Lost in the abyss of sleep, she faced me. Her blonde hair flowed out all around her, and a single lock dripped over her shoulder and brushed along her neck.

Peaceful. Perfect. Beautiful.

Forever beautiful.

I gently brushed my fingertips across the sharp angle of her jaw, then down to caress along the cap of her delicate shoulder.

Her lips parted, but she didn't awaken.

As I watched her, adoration lifted one side of my mouth, and I trailed my fingers farther to her left hand that was fisted on the bed, tucked up close to her face. The diamond on her finger caught a glimmer of light that slanted in from the rising sun outside the window. It danced and played, a symbol of our forever.

Tomorrow, this woman would finally be my wife.

How had I ever become so favored as this? Maybe I could call it luck. But I knew better than that. This was redemption. Elizabeth had saved me with her forgiveness, had saved me with her honest heart.

She'd given me back my family, and together, we would grow it, foster it. Foster us.

Joy pounded steadily in my chest.

No, things just didn't get any better than this.

I stared at her for a second more, before I

reluctantly untangled myself from the comfort of our twisted blanket and sheets. I stood and stretched my arms over my head, wishing I could crawl back in bed with Elizabeth and wake her up the way I really wanted to. I'd woken up with an intense urge to bury myself in her, to get lost in her body for hours and hours.

Instead I'd lain silently at her side and just listened to her breathe.

She needed her rest. She was feeling so much better than she did in the beginning, but that baby girl still took so much out of her. Today would be nonstop with the last minute wedding plans…and tomorrow…I just wanted her to feel well, to bask in it, for her wedding day to be perfect.

That's what I wanted it to be.

Perfection in Elizabeth's eyes.

I already knew it'd be perfection in mine simply because in it, Elizabeth would finally become my wife.

Nothing else mattered.

Casting one last smile at her sleeping form, I forced myself into the alcove bathroom and turned the shower on high. I stripped off my underwear and waited for the water to warm up. Steam began to spill over the top of the walk-in shower, and I stepped into the heated spray. I lifted my face to the flood of water and scrubbed my palms up through my hair as I drenched my body.

Exhilaration traveled beneath my skin, an excitement that buzzed in my bones. I couldn't wait.

After so long, I had finally made this *right*.

My senses prickled in awareness as I felt it…eyes tracing me from behind. Or maybe it was her smell that infiltrated my mind. Either way, Elizabeth's presence engulfed me.

Slowly I turned to look over my shoulder, blinking through the droplets of water that clung to my lashes.

And she was there, *my life*. Half her body was concealed as she braced herself on the outside of the shower wall, peering in at me. Her head was tipped to the side. Waves of dark blonde dripped over one shoulder and brushed across the swell of her perfect, round breast.

A muffled groan rumbled from somewhere deep in my chest as my attention raked down to relish in every exposed inch of her luscious skin.

Completely bare, Elizabeth stood before me.

I swallowed hard. "What are you doing, Elizabeth?"

She was still thin, though her hips were just a little fuller, and distinct lines cut into the muscles of her defined legs. And her stomach. Was it wrong that I found that bump the sexiest thing I'd ever seen? She wasn't all that big yet, but it was pronounced, a round swelling of her belly that fit perfectly in the splay of both of my hands.

She was watching me with something akin to lust, though that look harbored so much more than simple desire. In it was everything I felt when I looked at her.

Devotion and need. Adoration and this passion that would never let us go.

I grew hard, my body reacting to this temptation. I was all too happy to step into her snare.

"I woke up to an empty bed," she murmured in the most seductive way, in a way that only Elizabeth could because it was only her voice that I recognized. "And I don't get to sleep with you tonight...and...I just needed you," whispered from her mouth. She gently lifted her chin and dragged her fingertips down the soft slope of her neck. Her fingers fluttered as they trailed down to the valley between her breasts, beckoning me to look at her, to see her.

She was beautiful, unbelievably sexy. Every erotic flick of her fingers was enough to drive me mad.

My eyes made another pass over her body as she stood there, taunting me.

A rosy glow blossomed across her skin on my blatant perusal.

Uninhibited and *shy*.

This was where Elizabeth captured me, where I

was her captive, because I knew she'd only been this free with me, that this was the trust we shared.

An edgy smile pulled at my lips, and I fully turned so she could see what she did to me. Water pelted my back as I faced her, my erection straining, begging for her touch.

"You need me, huh?" I said, the words hoarse with the hunger that steadily built within me. "I'm pretty sure it's me who needs you."

A surprised moan rolled from her, and she bit at her lip and looked up at me beneath the veil of hair that had fallen across one side of her face. A mist of steam dampened her skin as she inched into the shower. Goosebumps visibly flashed across her flesh. Brown eyes locked on mine as she approached, her eyes simmering in a slow blaze.

With her stare, the burn beneath my skin ignited, flamed, a raging fire that singed and seared. Just her gaze was enough to mark me.

But Elizabeth already was there. Written all over my heart, scored into my spirit.

Watching me, she dragged her fingers lower, let them pass over her stomach and slip between her thighs.

My jaw clenched as my attention fastened on her movements. My tongue darted out to dampen my already wet lips, and my eyes flicked up to meet hers before they tumbled down, seeking out the tease she injected into every single one of her actions.

Fuck.

A muted groan parted my lips when Elizabeth raked her nails over the perfect pink bud of her breast. Both pebbled at the touch.

"What are you doing?" I asked again, the rough, ragged words dropping from my mouth, because I was pretty sure what she was doing was driving me straight to the edge. My muscles twitched, every inch of me aching for her.

She took a single step forward, where the fall of water stretched out just enough to hit her stomach. Soft fingers caressed along my chest and down the plane of my stomach, her chin tilted up as she met my gaze. Soft, tender, her expression so sweet, but still intense, filled with need.

Beneath her touch, my abdomen tightened and jumped.

She rocked a little, almost tentative as she took me in her hand.

I jerked and sucked in a sharp jolt of air.

"I woke up and heard the shower running," she murmured, never looking away. "All I could think about was you in here, the water falling all around you, every inch of you drenched in it, how beautiful you are." She swept her tongue across her lips, frowned as if she were searching for what to say. "I couldn't stop thinking about how you're finally really mine. All those times in college when you promised me you were going to marry me, and after everything, you still held true."

Shudders wracked through my senses as she guided her hand up then slowly back down again. We were nose-to-nose, her whispered words like an embrace as they washed across my face and her voice dropped low. "I wanted to touch you...wanted you to touch me."

A growl emanated from somewhere inside me, something that felt like greed, a possessiveness wringing me tight. Because we *belonged*. Fully. There were no longer uncertainties or doubts.

I wrapped my palm around the back of her neck and pulled her flush to me. My mouth seized hers, forceful, needy, demanding. I captured her tongue with mine, stroked and pleaded just as firmly as she continued to stroke me. Water beat down on us from above, soaking her hair and slipping down her gorgeous body. Goosebumps rose across her delicious flesh, charging my already heated skin.

"God, Elizabeth, do you have any idea what finding you standing here does to me?" I demanded through my aggressive kiss. I flattened myself against her as I framed her face in my hands. "Do you have any idea how insane you drive me?"

I looked down at her, feeling her warmth seeping into me, this girl who was the one.

She gripped me a little tighter. "It's no different

than what you do to me."

The buzz in my bones awakened, quickened to a roar. Emotion swelled, thickened as it traveled through my chest, evidence of this love that thrived, one that gave me breath.

I took both her hands and wrapped them around my neck, holding her close.

Elizabeth shook in my hold, and I moved to trail my nose from high up on her cheek and down. Nudging her jaw, I sought out the soft skin of her neck, kissed her, adored her, traveled up to suck at the sensitive flesh at the hollow of her ear. I nipped and bit, then brushed my lips across the reddened skin to soothe the burn.

My mouth found the lobe of her ear, and I drew it between my teeth, released it before I spoke, the words scraping up my throat.

"I woke up absolutely aching for you today, Elizabeth. You lying in bed with me, tempting me while you slept."

I slid my nose beneath her ear, nuzzled deep into her hair. I inhaled, drew her in, because she was the one who sustained my life.

"Did you know that? Did you know how badly I needed to feel you this morning? You drive me completely mad because it should be impossible that one woman could affect me this way." I pulled back an inch and pinned her with my stare. "Only you."

With my confession, her lips parted, brown eyes burning into mine. When she spoke, it was earnest, filled with truth.

"Only you…that's all there's ever been, Christian. You're all there will ever be."

An ardent smile curved her mouth—the same mouth I conquered with mine. My tongue swept over hers, urgent in its claim. She yielded to it, opening to me.

My hands roamed, skimming down the small of her back and to her bottom. I tipped her up and ground myself against her warm center.

Elizabeth gasped and buried her fingers in my hair. I took the opportunity to bend her back, dipped down to run my tongue along the rise of her breast. I sucked her nipple onto my mouth, rolled it against my tongue as I laved and teased.

She writhed.

Elizabeth suddenly dropped to her knees.

Fuck.

There was no stopping it, the desire that slammed me, knocked the breath from my lungs as she swirled her tongue around my tip before she took me whole.

"Shit, Elizabeth…" My head hit the shower wall. I grasped her by the head, my fingers buried in her hair. Pressing my thumbs into her jaw, I made a vain attempt to stop her assault.

But it just felt too damned good.

My hands picked up her rhythm, guiding her as she worked me into a frenzy that I was helpless to stop.

What she couldn't take of me in her mouth she took in her hand. And she was making all these little noises that were quickly pushing me to the brink, winding me up so fast I was about to break.

"Uh...that feels incredible," I grunted. Too good. Pleasure coiled. I needed to stop this before it was over before we even began. "Fuck," I hissed as I gripped her by the hair and slowly drew her back.

Elizabeth's needy eyes met mine as she reluctantly released me.

I was aching, hard, straining, burning to be inside her. I cupped her cheeks and forced her to stand, urged her up against the shower wall. Her back hit the tiles with a thud.

I sank two fingers deep inside her.

Elizabeth gasped, her head rocking back as she searched for air. Her body bowed, arching as if she were instinctively seeking me out, as desperate for my body as I was for hers. I hovered an inch over her with one hand pressed to the wall just above her head. My heavy erection begged where it slipped along the base of her belly.

"Please," she whispered. Elizabeth was shaking, her nails digging into my shoulders as I rushed to fill her again and again, my fingers curling inside her warmth.

I dropped my hand from above her head and edged back a fraction to let my hand wander along her belly. Elizabeth sagged against the wall, her stomach tightening beneath my touch as I splayed my hand wide, cupping the protrusion resting between us.

"This is so fucking sexy, Elizabeth. Do you know that? Watching you grow round with my child. There's nothing more beautiful than that. Nothing in this world more beautiful than you."

I felt her start to tremble at my words. "Christian…please."

Instead I slowed and raked my eyes down to where my hand was buried between her thighs. "Look at you," I demanded through a harsh whisper. Both of us watched as I slowly worked her with my fingers, purposed and strong, teasing her with release. But I refused to let her go. "Look at how perfect you are."

She shook more, and she reached out again to grasp me around the neck. "Christian, please, I can't take much more," she begged.

I pulled back, my hands on her hips as I looked down at her. I strained between us, dripping with need.

And those warm brown eyes were gazing up at me, overflowing with trust, with all the belief she had in me.

I took her by the thighs and hoisted her higher, filled her hard and fast.

A jagged breath squeezed from her lungs and her nails cut into the rigid muscles of my back. "Ugh," came as a grunt forced between her lips.

"Is this okay?" I begged through a grunt.

Shit.

My control was slipping by the second. But there was no chance in hell I'd hurt her. I locked gazes with her, my hand coming up to brush away the hair sticking to her face as the water ran down it. "Baby...tell me this is okay because it's been way too long since I've had you this way."

Both of my hands moved to her ass, where I gripped her, balancing her weight, my fingers teasing along her flesh where we were joined.

She moaned and tightened her legs around my waist. "Ah...perfect...don't even think about stopping."

And I was fighting a smile, this girl, this woman who was so incredibly sexy, so perfect, the one who anticipated what I needed before I asked for it, the one who knew me.

I pulled back and rocked into her again, hard, demanding. Her back slammed against the wall.

"Yeah?" I challenged, another test, just because I wanted to hear her say it.

"Yes," she said, giving me exactly what I wanted.

My hips jerked as I rocked into her. I filled her again and again. Relentless. Desperate. Because I would forever be desperate for her.

Incoherent pleas tumbled from her mouth, bled and blended with grunts scraping up my throat.

"Fuck...Elizabeth...you feel so good. Baby, I need more," I grated as I pinned her with my hips. Shifting, I wound my arms under her legs, held her by the back of the thighs. I stretched her wide and sank into her deeper than I ever had, forcing the air from her lungs with every thrust of my body.

I held her bottom in my hands, quickened as I drove into her.

Her eyes locked on mine as she tipped her chin up to me, our connection unshakable, the woman I held in my hands representing everything that was good in my life.

"More," she said.

She raked her fingers down my back, dragged them back up to anchor in my hair. And we were face to face, our mouths a breath apart. Short rasps of air escaped from her throat and she was staring at me as if I were her world.

The burn of pleasure tightened like a knot in my spine, pulsed as it begged to be set free.

"Christian...mmm...so close," she mumbled, struggling to get me closer.

I gripped her tighter as I tilted, rolled my hips and rocked into her. "Come for me," I demanded.

At my words, I felt it tear through her, ripping through her in staggered, palpable waves.

That was all it took, and I gave, snapped as I was hit with a pleasure greater than anything I'd ever known. It could only be found in Elizabeth. I throbbed and jerked as I came, my hips pinning her to the wall.

Gasping, I searched for breath as my chest collapsed against hers.

My fingers loosened their hold, and I gently wound my arm around her waist to hold her up. My smile bled soft as I looked at her. "That was…" I blinked, realizing there were no words. No words for this woman who was my heart, no words for the woman who held my soul.

Instead I brushed back the soaked hair matted to her face, gently tucked it behind her ear, and cupped the side of her face. I ran my thumb along the apple of her cheek. My throat bobbed heavily as I swallowed.

"I can't wait to call you my wife. You've been Elizabeth Ayers for far too long." My words were coarse with intent. "I'm going to give you everything, Elizabeth. Anything you want in this world, it's yours."

Her smile was almost sad as she looked at me. With trembling fingers, she reached out and traced my bottom lip. "That's all I want, Christian. All I want is to forever be yours."

FOUR MONTHS EARLIER, EARLY JUNE

Wracked, broken sobs beat into my chest where her face was buried. I stood at the side of the bed, bent over her as I cradled her head in the crook of my arm. My other arm was mashed between us, our hands clasped, clutching, searching for anything to ease this pain.

My head spun with confusion. A disordered chaos rained down like a raging storm, a flood sent to ruin and destroy.

Elizabeth clamped down on my hand as she wept. She pressed her face deeper into my shirt. Her mouth gaped open as she cried out, "No."

Dizziness swept through me. It amplified the shock that clung like a torpid haze to my muddled mind. A sharp stab of sickness twisted my gut, so strong it almost brought me to my knees.

No.

Elizabeth's doctor's voice broke through. "I know you don't want to do this, Elizabeth, but I need you to. Just one little push, okay? All we need is one tiny push and it'll all be over." Dr. Montieth coaxed her, the woman's tone sympathetic as she persuaded Elizabeth into succumbing to what she didn't want to do.

"I can't," Elizabeth wailed again. Her tears

soaked through my shirt as she wept against my chest. She squeezed my hand so tightly it constricted the blood flow, her fingernails cutting into the skin at the back of my hand.

I tightened my hold on her. I would give anything to stop this. Would give up my life, would give up my soul.

No.

Desperately I searched inside myself for a way to give her comfort. I wanted to tell her it would be all right. I tried to say it, but the lie only wedged in my throat.

It wouldn't be all right.

Instead I begged, "Shh...baby...shh," through a choked whisper at her ear, completely helpless. Utterly and completely helpless. Powerless to do a goddamned thing but stand here and watch our world fall apart.

"Yes, you can, Elizabeth. I need you to do this for me," Dr. Montieth prodded. Her voice was both soft and firm.

Elizabeth screamed as her body gave in. She cried out into my shirt that was drenched with her tears. I clutched her by the back of her head, held her closer, let her sobs tear and rend and destroy as they sliced though me.

Cold slipped through my veins as an anguished stillness seized the room.

Breaths were held in the second my heart broke.

God, I'd dreamed about this moment since the second Elizabeth and I had stood in her bathroom with that test, while joy had consumed us as we'd hoped for this future. Pages upon pages had been dog-eared in that fucking book I kept on my nightstand, the one I'd studied as if it were the Bible, so I'd be familiar with every detail. I wanted to be prepared to support Elizabeth, wanted to be prepared to welcome our little girl into this world.

But I never could have been prepared for this.

Absent were the cheers of encouragement. Absent was the rally of support. There was no urgent thrill and there was no joy radiating from these walls.

Instead, stifled air bore down from above, smothering, suffocating, a silence so thick it echoed from the cold, sterile floor.

It was penetrated only by the deep, agonized cries that ripped from Elizabeth.

In it was chaos, mayhem in my mind. Because I could make no sense of this.

Because it was senseless. Wrong. Unimaginable.

Part of me didn't want to see, the other couldn't look away. My hold was fierce as I clutched Elizabeth, keeping her face hidden in my chest as if I could shield her from the cruelty that played out before my eyes.

And there were no shrill cries that welcomed her into this world.

There was just an unbearable stillness and the most excruciating pain I'd ever experienced in my life.

On a disposable blue pad, Elizabeth's doctor held our lifeless child in her hands.

Blood stained her, covered her whole, this little girl that already held my heart. My vision blurred. She was so small. God, she was so small. So thin. The cord that was supposed to have sustained her life, but had instead snubbed it out, was still connected to her belly, still connected to Elizabeth.

Vomit pooled, and I forced it down as I stumbled through the fog that tumbled and whirled. Somewhere within myself, I fought for coherency, screamed at myself to wake up, because this had to be nightmare. There was no possible way that this was real.

Through the haze, I blinked down at my baby girl as they cut through her cord.

The nurse took her away while Dr. Montieth continued to work on Elizabeth, to birth the aftermath of our destruction.

And Elizabeth. She just cried. She just cried and cried and wouldn't stop, and I had no idea how to stop the pain.

I kissed her on the crown of her head. "I love you, Elizabeth," I whispered into her hair.

She clung to me a little tighter.

I glanced at the clock. It was just after two a.m.

It'd felt like seconds, like ages since this morning when it'd started with the promise of our future.

How had it ended this way?

Just like that.

Over.

Elizabeth had called me a little before noon. I'd answered with a smile, laughing with Matthew as we picked up our tuxes. But Elizabeth...the fear in her voice had struck me silent. She'd whispered that she was sure something was wrong. Hoping to assuage her fear, I told her not to worry and to call Dr. Montieth. Still, something inside me had quaked.

I knew I should have been gentler with her this morning, knew I'd been rough and demanding.

Knew if I'd hurt her I'd never forgive myself.

Dr. Montieth had told her to drink some orange juice, to lie down for a while and then to call her back if she still didn't feel Lillie move after half an hour.

That half hour had passed, and Elizabeth had called me, frantic, begging me to come home. I was already on my way.

We went into the emergency room where they sent us up to the maternity floor. Dr. Montieth had met us. She'd come into the room with the normal smile on her face. She had laughed a little, teasing Elizabeth that she was always worrying, her casual demeanor something that always set us both at ease.

Until I saw her face.

I saw it, the grim set of her mouth as she held that little probe at Elizabeth's belly, as she searched and searched and searched for a heartbeat that she told us later had probably stopped beating during the night before.

She thought it was a cord accident, although she said we couldn't be one hundred percent certain.

But in the end, it didn't matter because it didn't change the fact that our little girl was gone.

Dr. Montieth had given us our options. Elizabeth could be induced or she could go home and wait for her body to naturally go into labor. But the one option we wanted wasn't viable, the one that would give us the chance for this baby to live.

Neither Elizabeth nor I could bear the idea of going home and knowing that our child was gone.

And eight hours later, we were here.

Broken.

Elizabeth continued to cry, and I tried to breathe—tried to breathe for her as I hovered over her, hugging her to me, but it felt impossible, because there wasn't enough air for the both of us. Not enough for any of us.

My head pounded, throbbed and splintered, blinding, so severe I couldn't see.

Finally, Dr. Montieth finished the torture, but the torment had only begun.

Thirty minutes later, one of the nurses came back in. I edged back and stood at the head of the bed to give her room, so she could come to Elizabeth's side. Sympathy was written in every line on the woman's face, her voice subdued as she bent her knees and got to eye level with Elizabeth. "Would you like to hold her now?"

Through her tears, Elizabeth frantically nodded. "Yes."

She'd already decided this. Elizabeth wanted to see, to be given the chance to hold our baby girl.

"Okay, I'll be right back."

A few moments later, she returned. Lillie was completely wrapped in a blanket, her face covered. The nurse gently laid her in Elizabeth's arms.

An unrecognizable sound squeezed from Elizabeth, a pain so intense, it ricocheted around the room, reverberated off the walls, slammed into me. She cradled her on her shoulder, rocked her as she cried out toward the ceiling, as she cried out toward the heavens. It transformed into a desperate whine as Elizabeth slowly began to unwrap her, as she kissed her face and her fingers and her toes. Elizabeth felt her, touched her, a frenzy taking over Elizabeth as she memorize every inch of the little girl we would never really know.

I moved to sit in a chair beside Elizabeth's bed. I rested my elbows on my thighs with my hands dangling between my knees. I just gave Elizabeth time, because that was the only thing I had to give.

Elizabeth's mother came and went, touched my cheek as she passed.

Hours passed, and the sun slowly rose on what was supposed to be our wedding day.

And still I reeled, my thoughts unable to catch up to this savage reality.

All off it... I dropped my head toward the ground and buried my face in my hands. I could bear none of it.

There was a soft knock at the door. It opened so slowly, and I looked up just as my mother emerged. Tears stained her cheeks, her vivid blue eyes dimmed with the same agony that held my heart. She stood there, biting at her bottom lip as another round of tears streamed down her face. Her attention locked onto Elizabeth, who rocked the child, unwilling to let her go.

She approached, almost cautious, and eased down to sit on the edge of the bed. With her palm, she touched Elizabeth's face and drew it up to meet her own.

God, I had to look away. What was held in Elizabeth's expression tore me apart. She was shattered. Swollen, dark bags hung beneath her eyes. Those eyes were red, glassy, dazed, as if she couldn't make sense of this any more than I could. In all of it was agony.

Mom brushed her hair back and kissed her forehead. "You brave, wonderful girl," she said as she held Elizabeth by the chin, sitting back as her head drifted to the side. She never broke connection with the grief flowing from Elizabeth's gaze.

Finally she turned her attention to Lillie and, with her palm, cupped her tiny head. "Look at her...she's beautiful." Sorrow clotted her words, and she ran her thumb along the span of her forehead. "I know you don't need me to tell you this, but don't let anyone try to convince you this child is anything less than your daughter."

Mom unfolded an old blanket that she pulled from a bag and draped it across our child. "This belongs to her."

Elizabeth choked over a sob.

I averted my gaze to the ceiling. God, this was excruciating. Brutal.

Then she rose, touched her little hand, then placed another kiss to Elizabeth's head, let it linger like an embrace.

She turned and kissed me in almost the same way as she'd done Elizabeth, with actions that were full of understanding, with sympathy that I wasn't sure I could bear.

Then she quietly slipped out of the room.

Elizabeth's sister, Sarah, came in with the same result. Just more fucking sorrow heaped into this room that was becoming harder and harder to bear.

I yanked at my hair, feeling like I was seconds from losing my mind. I couldn't do this. Couldn't. I didn't want to. I wanted my daughter. I wanted Elizabeth to become my wife. I wanted to make this right.

And Elizabeth just held her, rocked her and kissed her and fucking talked to her.

Finally I couldn't take it any longer. "I'll be right back," I said.

I stumbled down the hall and found my way into the men's restroom that was just as fucking unbearably cold as the rest of the rooms of this godforsaken place. In its reprieve, I grabbed for the counter to hold myself up as I looked in the mirror. I was haggard. Black hair stuck up in every direction and dark circles sat prominent beneath my dismal eyes.

Anger shook me, and I clung to the edge of the counter as I bent at the waist.

How could this have happened? How? Today, Elizabeth was supposed to become my wife, and instead, we were here.

My head pounded with the pain, with the constant flashes of the life we were supposed to lead.

I turned as if I'd find escape, but just faced a wall. I dropped my forearms to it and rested my forehead against it, holding myself up as it all came crashing down.

"Fuck," I cried. My fist slammed into the hard, cold tile just beside my head. Pain splintered my bones, but it didn't come close to touching the pain that ravaged me in places I didn't know existed.

Ruined.

Destroyed.

Never had I believed anything could hurt this bad.

Hopelessness came barreling into my consciousness where it firmly took root.

I gasped for air.

But there was none to be found.

I forced myself to the sink and splashed cold water on my face. I couldn't do this. I knew Elizabeth needed me. I staggered back out into the hall.

Matthew leaned up against the wall outside of Elizabeth's room. His steady gaze met mine as I approached him. I dropped my eyes. Too many emotions tumbled through me, welling up and threatening to burst free.

He straightened as I approached, then pulled me in for a hug, just a clap on the back before something seemed to hit him, and his arms constricted around my shoulders. He hugged me hard.

"I'm sorry, Christian." He stepped back and looked to the far wall, rushed the back of his hand beneath one eye as he sniffled. "Fuck…I can't believe this happened. I don't even know what to say to you right now."

My chest tightened. I wondered if it'd always been this hard to breathe. "You don't need to say anything."

He turned to me with a nod, as if he perfectly grasped my meaning. Then he fixed his attention on me. "Elizabeth's Mom went back to our house to be with Lizzie, so Natalie could come over here. We were able to keep Lizzie satisfied last night, but she knows something's up. I can tell she's scared. She's starting to ask a bunch of questions and is whining. She's just not acting like herself. Do you want me or Natalie to talk to her?"

I shook my head as I stared at the gleaming white floor. "No. They're supposed to release Elizabeth a little later. Let me get her home and then I'll come and get Lizzie, okay? I want to be the one to tell her."

"Okay…I'll just let her know you'll be there to get her in a little while."

"I appreciate you looking out for her."

"Of course, Christian. Whatever you guys need…anything…just let us know." He ran a shaky hand over his head and down his neck. "I'm going to get back to the house, relieve Elizabeth's mom for a little while so she can come back over here."

"Thank you," I said sincerely.

"Please…Christian…please…don't let them take her." She was frantic, flailing.

I pinned her arms down, spoke close to her face. "Baby, it's time…you have to let her go."

"No!" She struggled against me, her cries like fucking torment beating against my ears.

My spirit thrashed, clashed with hers as she begged.

"You have to let her go," I said again, the words cracking as I forced them from my mouth.

Elizabeth wept, lifting her back off the bed as she bucked against me, her anguished face lifted toward the ceiling. Tears streaked from the creases of her eyes and slipped down to disappear in her hair. "No…please, Christian, don't let them take her."

"You have to, Elizabeth."

"Please," she whimpered. But this time, it was in surrender. Her body went limp and she slumped back onto the bed, but the tears from her eyes fell unending, her hands balled up in fists as my hands shackled her wrists.

I swallowed down the misery and slowly

released the hold I had on her wrists. "I'm so sorry," I whispered. It sounded like my own concession.

Elizabeth withdrew, turned her face from me, her eyes pinched shut. I tried to wrap her in my arms, but she rolled to her side with her back to me.

I stood there, staring down at her as she drew ragged breaths into her lungs.

I'd promised her anything. Had promised her everything.

But I was left with nothing to give.

Six hours later, I drove around the slumbering neighborhood. Night had fallen, the dull street lamps flooding muted light along the road. An hour before, Lizzie had fallen asleep in her booster in the backseat of my car. When I'd stood in the doorway to Matthew and Natalie's, looking down at my little black-haired girl, it was as if she'd already known. She looked up at me, stricken, grief swimming in the depths of her young eyes. I'd gathered her in my arms and took her to the park where I told her everything in as little detail as I could, though the images had raged, vivid violence playing out in my mind.

Now I drove, listening to my daughter's uneasy breaths emanating from the backseat. I went in circles. Aimless.

I guess I didn't go home because I knew things would never be the same.

Dr. Montieth had taken me aside and promised me there was nothing I could have done, there was nothing I could have changed that would have led to a different outcome other than the one we'd been given.

But I couldn't stop my mind from going there, from wandering, from wondering, from blaming. There had to have been something that could have changed this course. If I'd have just been gentler, more cautious, made her rest.

The rational side of me knew it wasn't my fault, but my heart just wanted to protect her.

Exhaustion began to set in. The fog that had blurred my thoughts was now blurring my eyes. I wound back around, inching by the front of the little house we shared before I pulled into the driveway. One dull light glowed from within, the house quiet, sadness radiating from the walls.

Carefully I gathered Lizzie from the backseat and cradled her in my arms. I trudged up the walkway. At the door, I shifted Lizzie to the side, fiddled with the knob and unlatched it. The door creaked as it slowly swung open.

My mother jerked up from where she sat on the couch, perching on the side. Her expression caught mine. Bleak. Broken. Just like the rest of us. Tears wet her cheeks, and she seemed almost frantic as she wiped them away, as if she didn't want me to find her that way. For a moment, I just looked at her, before she tilted her head to the side as if to say she understood, when I was sure there wasn't a single person in this world who could possibly understand what I was feeling. I nodded though, turned and mounted the stairs with Lizzie sleeping in my arms.

I didn't take her to her bed. I passed it by and carried her into our darkened room.

From where she lay on her side on the bed, Elizabeth's silhouette seemed to fill up the entire space, her grief stealing all the air from the room.

Quietly I edged forward and placed our daughter in the middle of our bed. The two faced each other, lost in sleep, their breaths short and ragged. I tucked the covers up under their chins. Elizabeth shifted. Her arm wound around Lizzie's waist and she tugged her near.

I just stood there in the shadows, in the blackness that consumed the walls, the blackness that consumed my heart. It echoed back the void. The loss.

I backed into the wall, slid down to the floor and pulled my knees to my aching chest.

The whirlwind had subsided. The storm cleared. And all that was left was the devastation that laid in its wake.

PRESENT DAY

I'd let her down. Even if there was nothing I could have done to stop it, it didn't change the fact that I wasn't able to save my Elizabeth from the pain. I couldn't. I'd been just as helpless as she was, and that was what I'd never wanted to be.

And I missed my baby girl. I missed her so much because the love I had for her was real.

I didn't think a single second would pass in my life without me regretting not holding her. For being too much of a coward to hold my daughter in my arms. That decision would forever haunt me.

Elizabeth couldn't even look at me after it happened. Somewhere inside me, I understood that it really wasn't me, but that seeing me was an echo of what we had lost.

That didn't mean it didn't hurt. It didn't mean there wasn't anger and issues that neither Elizabeth nor I had been strong enough to deal with.

Never once had we talked. We'd just let bitterness and resentment grow. Until that day when no words had been spared. When they'd been said when they shouldn't have. I didn't mean it. I'd lashed out when Elizabeth had cut me to the core, her words so brutal she may as well have kicked me in the stomach.

I turned on the faucet and splashed cold water on my face, grasped the counter and hung my head between my shoulders.

The hairs at my nape rose in awareness, an awareness taking hold as her calm slipped into the room. Slowly I turned my attention to the bathroom door where Lizzie stood in the doorway, peering in at me as she clung to the knob.

She blinked through knowing eyes. "Are you sad, Daddy?"

I trembled a smile as I took in the little girl who was my light.

Swallowing hard, I spoke, the words strangled as I forced them around the lump wedged in my throat. "Yeah, baby, Daddy is very, very sad."

She edged forward, cautious as she stole into the bathroom. She came up behind me and wrapped her arms around the back of my legs.

Slowly I turned around and leaned down to gather her in my arms, slid down to the floor and pulled her onto my lap.

Lizzie buried her head in my chest, and she choked, a sob winding from her palpitating chest. She expelled it in the collar of my shirt.

With the connection, with her sorrow, I let it go, let my unshed grief fill my eyes as I clung to my daughter. Rocking her, I lifted my face to the ceiling, felt the wetness seep onto my cheeks.

Little fingers burrowed into my sides. "I'm so

sad, too, Daddy."

On a heavy exhale, I ran my fingers through her hair and laid my cheek on top of her head. "I'm so sorry, baby girl. I'm so sorry you have to go through this with us. I love you so much…don't ever forget how much I love you."

She held me even tighter. "I just want you to come home."

"I know, princess, I do, too."

That's all I wanted.

I just wanted to go home.

thirteen

I tugged down the sleeves of my sweater and fisted the ends in my hands. Wrapping my arms around my knees, I drew them to my chest. My eyes fluttered closed as I turned my face to the warmth of the sun that sat high in the sky. A cool breeze gusted in, stirring up my hair and rustling through the leaves of the citrus trees that I had loved so much when I purchased this house.

From my perch on the patio chair that I'd dragged out into the middle of my backyard, I hugged my knees closer to my chest.

What had compelled me to come out here, I really didn't know. But it seemed as if I hadn't felt the sun in so long. The last four months, I'd been consumed by darkness. A prisoner to the shadows that screamed my despair.

Today I woke to an empty house, but I was unable to force myself back into the refuge of sleep. Lizzie had spent last night with Christian. I usually slept away the mornings she was gone, and I wouldn't rise until it was time to pick her up from school.

Today, when my eyes had flitted open, I was struck with all the pain that continually devoured me, the wounds within throbbing anew as each new morning seemed to cut them wide open.

But even as I was washed in that pain, I sensed something different. It was as if the emptiness inside me had whispered that I was missing something as the days blurred into nothingness. It was something that echoed the loneliness that ached from my broken spirit. But where before I'd given into it, had succumbed to the void that I'd accepted would always be the most prominent piece of my life, today I had the impulse to fill it. It was just a flicker, but it was there.

I will try.

I guess I'd enjoyed myself on Sunday, if that was even possible. The fresh air had almost made it easier to breathe. Almost. Breathing was the hardest part. Every intake of air was measured. Forced. As if life no longer came naturally.

But being there with Logan, Kelsey, and Lizzie had been simple. There was no pressure and there were no memories. When Logan made me laugh, it shocked me. It was as if my ears were hearing it tinkle from someone else's mouth, a sound I no longer recognized.

And he called me Liz.

Casual. Like nothing. As if he'd known me all my life. As if it really didn't matter all that much.

Christian never called me that. He always said my name as if it were his breath, as if it were a prayer, so much meaning held in the just the inflection of the word.

Maybe that was the problem between Christian and me. Maybe the connection that bound us was too overwhelming, too powerful, too much. Maybe a love that flamed so bright could only burn us into the ground. Maybe it was inevitable, our ruin. Maybe we'd already been set up for destruction, because something so strong made it inherently weak.

Because I knew I couldn't handle Christian right now. Couldn't handle the intensity of what he made me feel. He was like a burst of color behind my eyes that I couldn't distinguish, a ball in the pit of my stomach that felt like both dread and anticipation.

He was a reminder of everything that should be and what I couldn't have.

A symbol of what I had lost.

The hardest part was I didn't know if that feeling would ever change. If I could ever look at him and not be knocked from my feet by a torrent of sorrow.

I opened my eyes and let my gaze wander across the yard to the swing set he'd built about six months ago.

I'd tried to talk him out of it. I'd told him he was crazy and that we were trying to move and he could build one at the new house. But he just smiled that smile and said it didn't matter, and if Lizzie played on it for even one day, then it would be worth his effort.

And she had. She had played and played and played on it until she had abandoned it the day Christian had gone away. Since then it'd sat stagnant, like the wreckage of our decay.

Gathering my courage, I stood. The grass was damp, cool beneath my bare feet. I approached it tentatively, as if it were something sacred. I ran my fingertips up the smooth plastic of the slide then brushed my hand along the coated metal chains of the swing where Christian had spent hours upon hours teaching Lizzie how to pump her legs. I swallowed hard as I moved to stand behind the other, the infant swing Christian had so proudly hung *just in case* we were still living here when Lillie was old enough to use it.

My hand shook as I reached out and nudged it, giving it the slightest push. It creaked as it barely swayed. I pushed it again and closed my eyes and imagined her, what she would have been like had she been here.

Her face flashed, both the one I'd known and the one that I'd fantasized in my mind. The way she'd felt in my arms. She'd been so light, too light, so wrong. And still, I'd loved her. I'd loved her with all my heart and I'd poured it into her, praying that somehow she could feel it.

Pain clenched my heart, and tears welled in my eyes as what I'd known of her presence swept over me. I pressed my hand over my mouth as it all broke through.

Oh my God. I hurt. I hurt so bad, I didn't how to stand up under it. It was crushing. But today I let it, lifted my face to the sky as I let it rain down on me, as I let her *touch* me, a caress of her spirit as she passed by.

I'd had so many hopes for her life. And I could see her here, could imagine the way she'd have smiled, the sound of her laughter, because I *knew* her.

Because I knew her, and without her, I couldn't remember how to breathe. I was hit with another staggering wave. It bent me at my middle, and I clutched my stomach as I gulped for the cool fall air.

I missed *her.*

A sob tore up my throat. It was unstoppable.

I should have known better than this, letting it go, welcoming the remnants of her existence into this miserable life. Because I couldn't deal with it, but I couldn't keep myself from receiving the smallest portion of her light.

I staggered back into my house. The drapes remained pulled, the rooms darkened as I stumbled through the kitchen and into the family room. On the stairs, I held myself up on the railing, pulling myself forward, or maybe I was drawn.

I'd never been able to look before, even though I knew it was there. Before she went back to Virginia, Claire had kissed my forehead and told me it was there for me whenever I was ready. And I didn't know if I was ready. I didn't know if I ever would be. Four months had passed, and I knew one day I had to face this.

I will try.

I came to a standstill outside my bedroom door. Tears streamed, and I just stared. I still didn't know if I was brave enough to handle what was inside.

Brave.

The hoarse laughter that shook me was almost bitter. None of it was directed at Claire, even though she was the one who had proclaimed it.

There was no bravery found in me.

After they'd ripped her from my arms, I didn't even have the courage to open my eyes. I just wanted to seep away, bleed into the nothingness that my spirit called me into.

I will try.

With a trembling hand, I reached out and pushed on the door. It swung open to the room that served as my refuge yet haunted me at the same time. In it was Christian's presence, both the warmest light and the harshest freeze. It was here I'd loved him and here where I'd let him go. These walls still crawled with that anger, something that had boiled between us before it'd finally blown.

Part of me still hated him for it.

Sucking in a pained breath, I took a step inside. The loneliness I was met with every time I walked through this door encroached, wrapped me in a cloak of isolation, amplifying the void at the center of me that was getting harder and harder to bear.

I swallowed deeply as I shuffled across the floor. I came to stand at the entrance to my walk-in closet. A frenzy of nerves sped through my veins. I pushed them down and slowly opened the door. A dark, vacant hole stared back at me.

I fumbled for the light switch. Harsh light flooded the tiny space. I squinted, holding my hand up to shield it. Once my sight adjusted, I edged forward then dropped to my knees.

The box was on the top shelf, shoved back and hidden behind a stack of blankets in the far corner.

Discarded.

Like waste.

Agony twisted my heart, so tight I didn't know how it was possible for it to keep beating.

She would never be that way to me. Forgotten. Unwanted.

Rejected.

A shot of anger rumbled beneath the surface of my skin, resentment I was sure I would never shake.

I tugged on the box and pulled it down, got onto my knees in the middle of the closet floor. It was a large keepsake box, pink and floral and accented in ribbons. The kind designed to keep someone's most cherished memories.

I sat there for the longest time, staring at it through bleary eyes, searching inside myself for the courage I knew didn't exist.

I fisted my hands on my thighs. I blinked, and tears slipped down my cheeks and dripped from my chin. I sniffled and wiped them away.

I owed her this. Owed her this respect, owed her this act of adoration when my body hadn't been strong enough to protect hers. And maybe I owed it to myself, because it was her memory I clung to so desperately, and her memory that caused me my greatest pain.

Maybe I needed to see.

Something pushed me forward, and I lifted the lid from the box. For a moment, I froze, stricken by the items waiting inside. My chest quaked. I slowly set the lid aside.

Little remained of her, just the few things that had touched her life.

My jaw quivered, and I sank my teeth into my lower lip to try to stop it.

She hadn't even been given that. *Life*.

But to me, she had. She had lived because she lived in my heart.

The tiny identification bracelet that had been cut from her ankle lie on top. It was so small, so small it could have been a ring. A shudder trembled through my being. Did I forget how small she had really been? I picked it up and gently twisted the plastic band that had marked her stilled leg around my finger.

Tears resurfaced. I tried to bite them back, but they bled free. And I knew they would fall endless, ceaseless, even when my eyes were dry. Never would I stop grieving her. This love was eternal. My name was there, just under hers, and numbers were printed below that I knew somehow categorized her death. I let it curl around two fingers, held onto it as I dipped my other hand into the box. I pulled out the preemie Onesie my mother had bought from the hospital gift store for me to dress her in. It was the one she'd worn as Mom snapped three pictures of her in my arms. They were there too, the pictures, tucked inside a card, a merciless reminder of her face that was forever frozen in time.

Stifled air pressed down. I felt strangled, as if the life were slowly being squeezed out of me.

Seeing her this way, so clear, removed from the fog of that day, gutted me.

Stripped me bare.

How could I face this? When would it ever be okay?

It wouldn't.

Still, I held the pictures at my chest as I lifted my face toward the ceiling. The single bare bulb glared down, streaks of light glinting against my eyes that were squeezed closed. Tears continued to fall, and my anguished cries bounced around the confines of the tiny space.

I could barely suck in a ragged breath. It hurt as it expanded in my lungs.

By the time I set the pictures down on the floor and pulled the blanket Claire had given her from the box, I could barely see. I frantically pressed it to my nose, desperate to catch a suggestion of her. I held it close and inhaled the fabric, because it felt like the most tangible thing I had of her.

But that void...it just throbbed.

She'd taken a piece of me with her and left this

hollowed out place that I didn't know how to fill.

And it ached and stabbed and cut.

She was real. Didn't they understand that?

But I knew no one really could. No one could really understand the impact she'd made on my life. How she'd changed me inside.

Because she'd been real and my child and now she was gone.

Gone.

And it hurt. Oh my God, it hurt so badly, stretched me thin and compressed me tight, and I didn't know if I'd ever see through it.

My fingers curled in the blanket as I wept, as I cried out for the child I would do anything to hold in my arms again.

One token remained at the bottom of the box.

I still didn't know if I could bear to look at it.

No amount of time could heal it. No passage of days or months or years could erase the fact that she had never been given the chance to live.

Memories surfaced, ones that I had blocked through the shocked haze that held me under. Ones I still didn't want to remember. Somehow, I knew Christian had picked it out. Vague impressions slipped through my mind, the way he'd tried to hold me as he'd asked questions at my ear I didn't want to hear. I remembered this was what he'd wanted and somehow I'd agreed.

It was a small pewter cube.

It was different from anything I'd seen, different from anything I'd expected when Claire had told me it was there, but I knew it was her urn.

A delicate script was inscribed across the top.

Lillie Ann Davison
Forever In Our Hearts

There was no date.

He'd simply stated her time as *forever.*

And for a moment, all I could feel was Christian's grief. It broke over me in a crashing wave. I gasped as it knocked me forward, and I held myself up with one hand as I struggled to breathe.

Had I been unable to recognize it then? Or was I just imagining it now?

But it was strong. Overpowering. As overwhelming as the confusion he spun up in me.

I fought against the oppressive weight that suddenly crushed my shoulders.

I couldn't bear his sorrow, too.

I became frantic, picking up her things, pressing them to my face, to my nose, before I rushed to put her pictures and small things back into the box.

I thought…

I thought I could do this. I thought I was ready, but I realized then, I was not. I didn't know if I ever would be. I couldn't look at them because I didn't want to let her go, and somehow holding all of her things made me feel as if I was trying to. It was just so much easier to hold it all inside, to box it up with all these things that I wanted to treasure, even when they just seemed to cause me more pain.

Sobs racked through me as I folded her blanket and hurried to place it on top of everything else.

But I couldn't.

I couldn't let her go.

My pulse stuttered as everything slowed. My fingers curled into the fabric, and I cautiously drew the blanket back out. My eyes dropped closed as I held the satin trim at my cheek.

fourteen

Frantic.

I couldn't breathe.

No.

I clutched her to me, rocked her at my chest.

No.

"You have to let her go."

This was all I had of her, and they were trying to take it away.

I fought, fought for her as I crushed her to me.

I just needed a little longer. That's all I asked. Just a little longer.

I needed to remember, needed to feel.

This was all I had.

I begged.

Fingers dug into mine, pulling me apart, tearing her away.

"No!" It wept as a ragged scream as the place inside me that had been carved out for her was ripped wide open.

Oh my God. Oh my God.

That was all I had. Didn't they understand?

Pain slammed me from all sides, pushing in and pressing out, rending and severing and destroying. It all spread out in a consuming agony.

Subdued, quieted footsteps pierced the room as they resonated across the hard floor, fell silent as the door was opened then fell shut.

They took her.

It throbbed, this hollowness that swallowed me whole.

She was gone.

Then I felt his breath at my cheek, heard his voice as it prodded, seeking to penetrate my ears. *I'm sorry.*

I wanted to lash out at him, spit in his face.

He let them take her. He was the one who'd said it was time.

He forced me to cast her aside.

She was gone.

Gone.

Pain clamped down on my pelvis, and my breasts ached to feed.

There was no air.

I couldn't breathe.

SIX WEEKS LATER

"Mommy." My name floated from her mouth on a whisper. A tiny hand pressed to my face. "Mommy, are you awake?"

I forced my eyes open.

Grief surged in.

I fisted the sheet against me and struggled to focus on my little girl. On the mattress, she leaned on her forearms, her chin to the sheets. Wide eyes peered into mine, her face two inches from my nose.

Rapidly, I blinked.

Lizzie turned a grin up at me, as if seeing my eyes open was the best thing she'd ever witnessed.

"Hi, Mommy," she said.

"Hi, baby girl," I whispered back, my voice hoarse from lack of use.

"You wanna play? I got my tea party all set up, and you have a special spot." She smiled at me with wide, hopeful eyes.

I swallowed. The motion hurt. Everything hurt. My arms. My stomach. My head.

My soul.

My voice cracked. "Not today, baby." I mustered a smile and reached out to gently touch her chin.

Her face fell with disappointment. "You don't want to play any day," she contended, almost whining, so out of character for my little girl.

Guilt slashed, raking its claws down deep in my skin, cutting as it splayed me wide. The wounds wept. I wasn't strong enough for her. Wasn't strong enough for either of them.

"I'm sorry, baby, Mommy doesn't feel very well right now. Maybe a little bit later, okay?"

She nodded, watching me with an expression that read too much. She inched forward and placed a kiss on my forehead. "Okay, Mommy. Feel better."

I mashed my eyes closed as she backed away, held them as I listened to her withdraw from my room. The gush of stagnant air I'd been holding in my lungs left me as I heard her retreating down the hall.

Within the safety of my bed, I burrowed deeper, tried to snuff it all out. The pain, the voices that continually told me one day it would be okay, as they spoke words that meant nothing.

I'd almost dozed off when I felt it.

Anxiety ratcheted through me the second I felt him emerge behind me in the doorway. Sickness crawled, slithered along the wounds that dripped from the surface of my skin. I could sense him, his intent stare as it swept over me. What used to feel like a caress now felt like an intrusion.

I pressed my eyes tighter, pretending to be asleep, praying that he would just leave.

I couldn't handle him. Couldn't handle his scrutiny, couldn't handle the way he looked at me as if he understood.

I couldn't stomach the anger.

"Elizabeth." My name from his tongue was frustration and sympathy and raging disappointment. "You can't keep doing this. Your daughter needs you. You need to get out of that bed." His voice softened in appeal. "Baby, get up…let's spend the day with Lizzie. Let's go to the beach…do something."

I stilled myself, trying to hold in the sob that rattled in my throat. If I just held fast long enough, he would go away. He would give up.

He would leave me.

This time, that's what I wanted him to do.

When I didn't respond, he released a frayed breath. "God damn it, Elizabeth, I know you're awake. Stop ignoring me. You've been ignoring me for weeks." He hesitated before he continued. *"Please."*

I swallowed hard, curled in tighter on myself, couldn't stand the sound of his voice landing against my ears. In my mind, I begged for him to just go. I couldn't do this with him.

But he just stood there. I could feel his eyes burning a hole into me. Subdued footsteps began to slowly move across the room, and he came around to my side of the bed.

Cold gripped me as he approached.

This was the man I thought I was going to love for all my life.

Even under the piles of blankets, I still felt frozen from the inside out. My pulse stuttered as I searched for the breath I could never seem to find.

A too-warm hand pressed to my ice-cold cheek. I tried not to cringe, but I couldn't stop the anxiety from seizing me, from yanking at my heart and sinking like a rock to the pit of my stomach.

I gagged when he ran his thumb under my eye, his breath spreading over my face.

"Baby, you have to get up. You've been in this bed for six weeks. We need you."

I flinched and jerked my face away.

Frustration left him in a weighted huff, his voice tight. "Damn it, Elizabeth, you have to get out of this bed. We can't do this any longer."

"Please, just leave me alone," I begged, turning my face the other direction.

"I'm not going to leave you alone any longer. I've let you lie here and lie here, and nothing is going to change until you *make* a change. I know you're hurting, but you have to do something different than this."

Until I make a change?

A fresh charge of anger needled into my senses, pricking as pain in the deepest places of my soul. "Just leave me alone." The words were hard, hoarse as they scraped up my dry throat.

He shot off the edge of the bed, and I buried my face deeper in my pillow and pulled the blanket over my head, praying for him to leave. I just wanted to sleep. Still, I could feel him pacing, could almost see him tugging at his hair as he stormed around our room.

I jumped when he tore the blanket from my face, and I jerked around to stare up at the man who I wasn't sure I recognized any longer. He was raging, his jaw clenched as he glared down at me as if I made him sick.

Or maybe it was the other way around.

And I felt it, something well in the air that made it harder to breathe than it already was.

"Elizabeth, baby, *it's time.*"

Flashes of them ripping my little girl from my arms slammed me, Christian making me, telling me it was *time.*

It's time.

It clattered around in the bowels of my brain. Memories. That day. What he forced me to do.

A roil of too many emotions boiled in my

blood. Burst free.

I pushed to my hands and knees. The effort took just about all I had. My head sagged between my arms, and I struggled to lift it as I leveled my eyes on Christian.

"Just leave me alone." All the bitterness I'd been feeling manifested on my tongue. "Just leave me alone! You have no idea what I'm going through."

"How can you say that?" he shot back. A deep line dented his brow. "You think I don't understand what you're feeling?" he demanded in sheer disbelief.

Incredulous laughter shot from my mouth in a contemptuous scoff. "What do you mean, how can I say that?" I pushed from my hands, sitting all the way up on my knees. "I was the one who carried her, Christian." I jabbed my finger to my chest. "I was the one who loved her and cared for her. She died inside of me, and I had to give birth to her." I lifted my chin. "So yeah, I can say that…you have no idea what I'm feeling. *None.*"

His entire face twisted in contention. "You think she meant less to me than to you? You think my heart isn't broken over this?"

"You wouldn't even touch her." It dripped from my mouth as a sneer.

He blanched, like I'd just slapped him across the face.

Maybe I wanted to. I had to admit I did. I

wanted to hit him, to pound whatever feeble excuse he had out of him. To demand to know how he could reject her that way. Our baby girl. The child we'd created. All those excruciating hours I'd held and rocked her, that I'd shown her all the love I possibly could before I wouldn't be allowed to anymore, he never even looked at her.

All that time I'd tried to love her for the both of us.

If it was possible, it'd broken me a little more.

Then he let them take her before I was ready to let her go. I begged him for one more hour. Just one more hour and he couldn't even give me that.

His entire body shook, and he blinked as if he couldn't believe what I'd said. "You think because I didn't *hold* her, I didn't *love* her?" His raised, caustic voice bounced against the walls.

Mine was low, but held all the sting. "I know you didn't."

Agony contorted his face.

"Just go." This time I choked, a sob breaking free because I couldn't understand what was coming from me, but I couldn't stop it. I was so hurt, so hurt. "I don't want you here."

He dropped his head and shook it, harsh and severe, as if he were grappling to make sense of what I had said. When he raised his attention back to me, fury flamed in his eyes.

"That's what you want?" he shouted as he flung

his hand out in my direction.

Raging, he stormed to the closet and tore the door open. It slammed back against the wall. Christian fumbled around inside and threw a suitcase into the middle of the bedroom floor. It tumbled, the lid flopping open as it settled. He began ripping shirts from their hangers and throwing them inside. He stalked back out, fisting a handful of shirts out in front of him.

"Is this what you want, Elizabeth? You want me to leave? You think I don't understand what you're feeling? You think you're the only one who has to go through this? You think you're the only person who's hurting? Then fine, do it alone."

I was gasping, crying, because his words flew out at me in a constant assault. I couldn't stop the slaughter, the way they took hold and destroyed the last piece of me.

He jerked the bottom dresser drawer open, pulled all his jeans out and shoved them into the suitcase. He glanced up at me as he ripped the zipper closed.

"I thought better of you than this, Elizabeth, but I was wrong. You are the most selfish person I've ever met."

I felt sick, an ache I couldn't understand gutting me. Still the words trembled from my mouth. "I hate you." I said it through choked tears.

I'd told him it before. This was the first time he

looked like he believed it.

It was the first time I thought maybe I meant it.

He leveled his gaze on me as he hefted the suitcase up by the handle. "Yeah, that's pretty obvious."

He started across the floor. Pausing in the doorway, he looked at me from over his shoulder. His throat bobbed heavily as he swallowed.

"Think whatever you want, Elizabeth, but I loved her. I loved her with all my life."

I watched him go, and I didn't try to stop him.

Instead, I wept, clutching my blanket to my face as I crumbled. My ears stung as I listened to him talking, his voice giving instructions to Lizzie. I couldn't make them out. They were muffled as I buried myself deeper in the refuge of the bed. I begged for the darkness that sleep would bring.

All I wanted was to go there.

All I wanted was to escape.

PRESENT DAY

I desperately sucked at the stifled air. It hurt as it expanded in my lungs. Everything still hurt so badly. I missed her. That hollow void ached for her, and I knew it always would. I pressed the blanket to my face. Confused tears fell when I realized I found some kind of comfort in it. It was small, but just like the urge to fill the void had flickered this morning, it was there.

I rubbed the satiny edge of the blanket against my cheek, the one that Claire had once held Christian in. Memories of him ignited in every one of my senses.

Affection sparked. I pushed it down, stamped it out. Forgiving him, moving on from this, seemed impossible.

It just hurt too much.

That day, Christian had gone, and he'd taken Lizzie with him. At the time, I'd been relieved, relieved that my little girl had been led out my door because I didn't have the strength to be the parent she needed me to be. Afterward, I'd slept for three straight days. I had never fully awakened until I'd been roused by Matthew sitting on the side of my bed, running his hand through my matted hair as he coaxed me from sleep. He said Christian had asked him to come check on me.

Christian had facilitated it then, Lizzie coming over to spend time with me. Through Matthew, he'd said Lizzie needed to see me. It was like I was being granted visitation, because I wasn't competent to take care of my own daughter. Knowing Lizzie would be coming home had been the only thing that had finally forced me out of bed.

We slowly slipped into a routine. Lizzie would

be at my house for a couple of days and then she'd spend a couple at Christian's, though when school had started again, she began spending more time at my place. Still, Christian had insisted he come and pick her up each morning for school.

For my daughter, I'd done my best to be up as much as I could when she was here, though half the time, I felt only partially conscious. The rest of the time, I slept away.

Guilt throbbed within me. For all these months, I'd felt a sense of relief while Lizzie was gone, relieved because I could just succumb.

I realized this morning, in the vacant emptiness of my room, that I was no longer relieved.

I missed her, and she needed me.

I will try.

Lifting my face to the ceiling, where the single bulb glared, I inhaled deeply as tears continued to stream from my eyes.

And for the first time in weeks, I wanted something other than to sleep.

I wanted to breathe.

fifteen

On Friday morning, I pulled into Elizabeth's driveway to pick Lizzie up for school and put the car in park. Still gripping the steering wheel, I stared at nothing through the windshield. Agitation curled through my consciousness. My leg bounced. God, I was about to lose it.

After what Lizzie had revealed to me Monday night, a sense of desperation had taken over. I'd been backed against a wall. Pinned as I watched the clock spin away. I was running out of time. I knew it. Felt it. If I didn't do something, I was really going to lose Elizabeth. The woman I would love for all my life. The woman who belonged to me, even if she no longer knew how to give herself to me.

Tuesday night, after I knew Lizzie would be in bed, I came here. I paced outside Elizabeth's door like some kind of obsessed stalker. But I was obsessed, obsessed with taking back my family. I couldn't let them slip away. That realization had given me the nerve to ring the doorbell. I knew she was standing on the other side of the door. I knew she was there, willing me to leave. And I just stood there. Waiting. Waiting for her. The way I'd been waiting for her all these months.

The longest time passed before the door had finally swung open. Her attention had been trained on the ground, her hair falling all around her as she'd hidden her face from me.

I'd stooped down and peered up at her, trying to capture her gaze, to finally make her *see*. I needed her to look, to *remember*.

I'd whispered her name. *Elizabeth*. In her name was everything I felt, the devotion to her that would forever consume my life, the wounds that still ached, and the striking need to feel her touch that would never leave me.

In it was all of my love.

God, how much did I love the broken woman who'd stood in front of me?

For one second, she'd given in and had met my gaze with a shakiness that wouldn't seem to let her go.

Wide, intense eyes stared at me from across her threshold. It was the shortest blip of time, but in it, we'd been frozen, as if the lives we were supposed to be living played in fast forward between us. Or maybe it was on rewind.

Just as soon as she opened her eyes to me, they'd slammed closed, shut it off, blocked me out. She flinched back, as if looking at me caused her physical pain.

Who knew one expression could cut me so deep?

Still, I'd pressed on, pushed her. "We need to talk," I'd said, stretching out a hand that so desperately wanted to touch her. But I'd held it back, knew I could only ask her for so much.

"I can't." Her voice was laced in agony. Apparently even that was asking her for too much.

But those two words had lacked all the venom that had filled the last real interaction we'd had, even if the result of them had still been brutal. Elizabeth, once again, shut down my efforts.

Every spoken word since I first left her house had been uttered with zero emotion, just plans made between us for our daughter. Nothing more.

This had been more.

"Please," I'd said with my heart feeling as if the

life was being squeezed out of it. "I can't let us go, Elizabeth. Talk to me. Tell me."

She'd shaken her head, whispered, "I'm so sorry." Tears clogged the words, and she stumbled over a pained, "I can't." Then she stepped back and closed her door.

I'd stood on the other side of it for minutes, maybe hours, having no idea what direction to turn. Did I force her, risk the possibility of things escalating, blowing up the way they had the day I left? Did I risk having her *say* it, Elizabeth telling me she no longer loved me?

But even if she said it, I wouldn't believe her.

I saw it in that one second she opened those brown eyes to me. She still belonged to me. Even if she couldn't see it.

I exhaled, heavy and hard, shut off my car, and climbed out. I plodded up her sidewalk and rang the doorbell.

A few seconds later, the door swung open to Elizabeth.

My breath caught.

It didn't matter how many days I'd stood at her door to pick up our daughter, it was always the same.

Intense longing exploded at my ribs, something that spoke of the regrets that would forever haunt my life, and the hopes that still flamed for my future. Elizabeth was in every single one of them.

Urges slammed me, ones that shouted for me to reach out, to take her. To do *something*.

Instead, I stepped back, gave her the space she demanded that was getting harder and harder to afford.

"Good morning, Elizabeth," I said, something I'd done all week, something that felt like progress, even though it was the most pathetic show of it.

At least I opened my mouth.

I bit back the incredulous laughter that stirred in my chest.

Pathetic was right.

I knew I had to do something, but I was pinned against that wall, and I didn't know how to break from it. How did I push back? How did I mount a battle when she wouldn't allow me the chance to fight for her?

She cast me a wary glance. "Good morning," slipped from her cautious lips. Then she turned away, looked toward the stairs, the way she did every morning. "Lizzie, sweetheart, your daddy is here."

"Coming."

This morning, Lizzie immediately appeared, her grin wider than I'd seen in so long. She rushed downstairs and ran to throw her arms around me. "Good morning, Daddy!" Excitement buzzed from her as she bounced.

A chuckle escaped me as I hugged her back.

"Well, isn't someone happy this morning."

She lifted that sweet face to me as she hugged me around my waist. "I get to go to my first sleepover tonight!"

Curious, I turned my attention to Elizabeth.

She was smiling down at Lizzie. Really smiling. Then she peeked up at me. "I was going to talk to you about that this morning and make sure you were okay with it. Lizzie was invited to spend the night at Adriana's house tonight for her birthday. I figured you wouldn't mind since she was going to stay here tonight anyway."

Lizzie jumped up and down. "Oh please, Daddy...I really really really wanna go!"

I laughed a little harder and ruffled a hand in her hair. "Well, I guess if you really really really want to go, I'll have to let you," I teased.

"Yay! Thank you, Daddy!"

She turned around and barreled into Elizabeth, squeezing her around the waist in a fierce hug. "Thank you, Mommy!"

Gentle laughter seeped from Elizabeth. "Of course, sweetheart." Then Elizabeth softened into the embrace, her hold tight as she clutched Lizzie to her, then stroked an affectionate hand through the long locks of Lizzie's hair. Palpable emotion swelled between them. "You have a fantastic day, my sweet girl. I'll be thinking about you."

Lizzie had her face buried in her mother's

stomach, the words muffled as she hugged her a little closer. "Okay, I will."

I drew in a faltering breath. Thankfulness surged. God, seeing the two of them like this, the love shared between them, it was as if it healed a small piece of the wounds still smoldering inside me.

With a soft smile, Elizabeth nudged her back. "Go on or you'll be late."

Turning, Lizzie rushed out into the day. "Let's go, Daddy!" She grabbed my hand and began to lead me down the walkway. Still lost in the sensations that had swirled between my girls, I hazarded a glance over my shoulder. Elizabeth watched us go. For the first time, she didn't look away.

I slowed to a stop, just before we rounded the corner to the driveway. I stared at the woman I was so desperate to put back together. Still, I was at a loss at how to do it.

Unmistakable sadness poured between us. All I wanted to do was turn around and take her in my arms, touch her face, kiss her. Love her.

Unaware, Lizzie tugged at my hand. "We gotta hurry."

Elizabeth blinked and the wall was back up.

With a resigned sigh, I turned and followed Lizzie to the car.

Five minutes later, I pulled to the curb in the

circular drive in front of Lizzie's school. She jumped out the back door and onto the sidewalk just as I came around the front of the car. Crouching down, I helped her slip her backpack onto her shoulders. I dropped a quick kiss to her forehead. "Have a great day, sweetheart. I hope you have a great time at your sleepover."

A dimpled grin split her face. "It's going to be the best day ever."

Warmth seeped into my skin, my little girl, my light. When it seemed impossible to smile, somehow this child made it unstoppable. I cupped her cheek, tilted my head with the force of that smile. "You'd better hurry. We're running a little bit late today."

She turned and jogged off.

"See you tomorrow," I called.

"See you tomorrow!" she sang as she looked at me over her shoulder.

I lifted my hand in a pensive wave. She headed back toward the entrance. She veered when she saw Kelsey standing beside her dad's car at the curb.

Every muscle in my body constricted.

Lizzie came to a stop at Kelsey's side. From a distance, I watched her tip her head back and laugh unrestrained. And that asshole was there, laughing, too. Then the piece of shit reached out and ran his fingers through my daughter's hair.

Motherfucker.

My hands clenched into fists at my side in the same second he glanced up to catch my stare. He turned back to Lizzie and Kelsey, said something else before the two rushed toward the school gates.

Anger curled, wound with the possessiveness that spun me into a frenzy. My head pounded, and I was pretty sure I was close to losing my mind.

Lizzie's words of last week blared into my senses, how excited she'd been, how much fun they'd had.

And Elizabeth had been different. Happy? Almost. Maybe. I shook my head. I didn't know. But definitely different.

Fuck.

I raked a shaky hand through my hair.

Was she seeing him?

I cut my eye back to him, searching for some kind of indication. A sign.

Had he touched her?

Images of Elizabeth with Logan crashed into my consciousness, clashing with everything I knew as right. I couldn't bear it. I squeezed my eyes closed to block them out.

When I opened them, he was gone, and I was left standing there like the fool I'd been all these months, staring at the spot where he'd been.

I moved to my car, my feet heavy, weighted, as if I were wading upstream, losing my balance as I got caught in the undertow.

My head spun.

Blindly, I drove to my office. I clicked my door shut behind me, sank into my desk chair, and stared out at the sailboats that bobbed in the bay as I tried to mentally plough through the mess that had become my life. Tried to make sense of it all. That anger just surged, stoked a jealous rage inside of me.

Would Elizabeth really do this to me? To us?

God, I couldn't imagine touching another woman. Ever. Not after Elizabeth had touched me the way she had.

The morning passed in a haze. A heavy fog swirled through my head. It contradicted the distinct itch I had bolt, to get the hell out of the suffocating confines of my office. When I couldn't tolerate it any longer, I rushed out, told my secretary I would be back soon, and got in my car and drove. The destination was clear, though I had no idea what I would say when I got there.

The only thing I knew was I couldn't let her go.

I pulled up to the curb in front of her house. Midday sun glared down from the sky, cast glinting rays through the windshield. The myrtle trees rustled in the gentle breeze. The little house looked so quaint, so quiet.

No one would have a clue of the pain we'd harbored here.

Sucking in a few resolved breaths, I pushed down all the anxiety of the unknown. All I knew was I had to talk with her, to lay it all out. I needed to tell her I loved her, and I could no longer go on living without her. Convince her she needed me as much as I needed her.

Leaving my car on the street, I ran up the sidewalk and pounded on her door. Agitation prickled at my nerves, and I scrubbed my palms over my face. Waiting, I paced.

"Come on, Elizabeth," I begged below my breath.

But there was no answer, no rustling or movement from inside.

Undaunted, I pressed my face to the window to the left of the door, peered inside at the stillness of the family room. A load of laundry lay in an unfolded heap on the couch, toys strewn across the floor.

She was probably in bed, the way she always was, hiding from the realities she didn't want to face.

Maybe I'd been wrong before. Maybe I'd pushed her into something she wasn't ready for.

But now…there was no question.

It was time.

I pushed past the boundaries that had silently been set. Fumbling with my keys, I produced the one I hadn't used in so long. Metal scraped as I slid the key into the lock. I pushed the door open to the silence that echoed back. Swallowing down the lingering reservations, I headed upstairs.

Our bedroom door sat just ajar. A slit of sunlight burst through the crack and shined against the hall wall.

I edged forward, cautious, and quietly called her name. God, I'd probably scare the hell out of her, sneaking up on her like this, waking her from sleep.

But there was no response, just more silence.

I touched the door. It creaked open. Her bed was unmade and empty. I inched forward, listening for movement from the bathroom. There was none.

Shit.

My movements were almost frantic as my attention shot around the room.

She was gone.

Elizabeth was never gone. I'd always banked on this, that she was lost in sleep, and that one day, she would *wake*. Fear gripped me when I realized she already had.

I just didn't know what she'd awakened to, where her heart had found her.

I ran downstairs, searched the rest of the house, peered into the backyard to no avail.

She was gone.

I ran back out front. On the sidewalk, I came to

a standstill. My hair flitted around my face as the wind came up, stirred along the ground, whipping up the fallen leaves.

What the hell was I supposed to do?

I pulled my cell phone from my pocket, scrolled through, called her. She didn't answer.

I left no message. This needed to be done face-to-face.

It was hell forcing myself back to go back to the office for an afternoon meeting I had. I was pointless, really. There was no focus, just images of her, the need that steadily built in my gut. The only thing I could see was Elizabeth. My life.

The second the meeting was adjourned, I headed straight for the door. I drove, my mind reeling and my heart pounding.

I couldn't let this happen.

I wouldn't.

This was my *family*. A family I'd always promised I'd fight for. That I'd live for.

Monday night had made me realize I wasn't.

No more. I refused to sit stagnant. I wouldn't let what was most important to me be ripped away.

I wouldn't let him have them.

I jerked my car to a stop in front of Natalie and Matthew's house. I jumped out.

What I was doing here, I didn't really know. But other than me, Matthew and Natalie knew Elizabeth best. They'd taken care of her through the roughest times in her life.

This, it was the greatest tragedy either of us had ever faced. She had to have gone to them. Another shot of jealousy hit me. I wanted to be that person, the one Elizabeth turned to in her time of need. How had we pushed each other away when we needed each other most?

I banged at their door.

Movement rustled from the other side, and the door opened to Matthew. Uncertainty lined every inch of his face, his eyes narrowed in distinct concern as he took in the mess that had to be my expression. "Christian...hey, man. Are you okay?" He peered behind me as if he were looking for an explanation before he turned his focus back on me. "What's going on?"

I shouldered by him and began to pace in the small entryway just inside their house. Every second that passed, I felt myself crumbling, my spirit thrashing, my control slipping a little closer to the edge. I tore at my hair before I looked back at the disquiet that had taken over Matthew's entire demeanor.

He placed placating hands out in front of him. "Hey man, I don't know what's going on, but you need to cool off. You look like you're about five seconds from having a coronary."

I blinked, swallowed, tried to rein it in. It left me in a ragged exhale that trembled through my chest.

"Is she seeing him?" I demanded.

I felt Natalie's presence emerge behind me at the end of the hall.

"Who?" True confusion seemed to saturate Matthew. He let the door swing shut as he turned to fully face me. "What are you talking about, Christian?"

I shot a glance at Natalie, who squirmed, restless as she pressed her hand to the wall, as if she were holding herself up. Uncertainty washed her face as she frowned.

I jerked my attention back to Matthew. "You two need to tell me what is going on with Elizabeth. Is she seeing that asshole? And don't lie to me."

Just the notion sent another shudder convulsing through my veins.

Was she sleeping with him?

I choked over the thought. Nausea rolled in my stomach. I was coming unhinged.

"Christian, come on, man, take a breath or something. Settle down for a second, because I don't have a single clue what you're talking about."

"Logan...Kelsey's dad," I clarified through hardened words. "Lizzie said Elizabeth has been over there, and I went over to Elizabeth's to talk to her earlier today and she wasn't home. She's *always* home."

Something like a smirk crested Matthew's

mouth. "Well, it's about fucking time. I take it back...don't calm down, because you've been sitting on your ass for far too long. It's about time you fought for her."

Natalie approached and placed a gentle hand on my back. "Why don't we go sit on the couch?"

I didn't resist, and I let her lead me around into their family room. I sank down onto the couch and buried my face in my hands.

Matthew plopped down in the recliner next to the couch, sat hunched over with his hands clasped between his knees.

Natalie settled beside me. Sorrow rolled from her, washed over me in burdened waves. A supportive hand found my knee. She squeezed it. "Tell us what's going on."

I raked my hands from my hair to my neck, blowing out a weighted breath. "I don't know...I just..." I cut my eye to Natalie, looked at her in all honesty. Brown eyes, so much like Elizabeth's, blinked back at me. Emotion tightened my throat. I could barely speak.

"I've been *waiting* for her, Nat. Waiting for something to change, for *her* to make a change." I raised my face to the ceiling. "I never once thought she'd make a change that didn't include me. But this guy...he said something a couple of weeks ago, and I just got this *feeling*." My mouth set in a grim line when I looked back at her. "Then on

Monday, Lizzie told me she and Elizabeth had gone over there for a barbecue. Of course, to Lizzie, it was all in fun, but I know something's going on."

Speculation twisted Natalie's expression, like what I'd said was an impossibility. I hoped to hell it was. "Do you *know* something is going on? Or do you *think* something is going on?" she asked.

In frustration, I drummed my fist to my forehead. "I don't know...it's just one of those things that hit me, you know?"

"Damn it." Matthew scrubbed his palm over his face as if he didn't want to believe it either. "Did you talk to her about it?"

"I've *tried*. I went over there on Tuesday and she said she couldn't talk to me. I knew I had to get through to her, so I went back today, but she was *gone*." I turned to Natalie, looking for some kind of reassurance. For her to tell me *something*. "She's different, Nat. I can see it."

Natalie's voice was low, cautious. "You know I'd never lie to you, Christian, and I promise you, she's never mentioned anything about this guy. But she hasn't really talked to me about anything. I made her come out to lunch with us a couple weeks ago, and she had a meltdown right in the middle of the restaurant. But in the car..." She worked her jaw as she seemed to think back. "I thought maybe I'd gotten through to her. I told her it was time, and she promised me she would try."

It is time.

Those three words. Who knew they could be so destructive? Every time they were said, I lost a little more.

Hopelessly, I searched Natalie's face. "What does that mean, she's going to try?"

She shook her head, her words subdued with regret. "I honestly don't know. But I'm worried she's not capable of making the right decisions in her current state of mind. She can't see through her grief, and I have no idea what's really going on in her head. But the one thing I do know is the two of you belong together. Nothing is going to be right for either of you until you are."

Matthew leaned forward, sitting on the very edge of his seat. "If she really is messing around with this guy, is it going to change anything? I mean, fuck, Christian." His gaze fell on Natalie who fidgeted at my side. Adoration filled his eyes. His head slowly shook as he turned back to me. "I can't even begin to imagine what you and Elizabeth have gone through, but I can guarantee you if I did, I wouldn't stop until I got Natalie back."

Tremors shook me, and I dropped my attention to the floor. Would it change the way I felt? Knowing she'd been with someone else? I swallowed hard. It would kill me. God, could I see through it?

Sitting back, I laid my head on the back of the couch as I crammed the heels of my hands against my eyes. A tortured groan flooded from my open mouth. "What the hell am I supposed to do?"

But I already knew the answer to that. There was only one.

I had to get her back.

sixteen

"Are you ready, sweetie?" I leaned on the doorframe of Lizzie's room and crossed my arms over my chest as I watched my daughter pack for her first sleepover.

"Almost…I just gotta get my toothbrush." She was on her knees, stuffing her backpack full of things I was sure she really didn't need—Barbies and little dolls, markers and stickers, and about different pairs of shoes.

Amusement tugged at me. This little girl was just too cute. I bit back my laughter as she struggled to close her zipper. "Do you really think you need to take all those dolls with you?" I asked.

"Uh-huh. Adriana has the same kind and we're going to play with them *all* night," she drew out.

I was betting she'd be asleep by ten.

She clamored to her feet, her little legs taking her as fast as they could as she rushed by me into the hall. I heard her digging through the drawer in her bathroom. She was back in seconds. She stuffed her toothbrush case into the side pocket, slung her backpack on her back, and grabbed her pink sleeping bag. She grinned as she rocked back on her heels. "All ready!"

"All right, let's get you over there."

She raced downstairs, and I followed her out into the cool evening air. I raised the garage door, and Lizzie climbed into the backseat of my car. I backed out and put the car in drive, couldn't stop my smile as I glanced at my over-eager daughter through the rearview mirror. A suggestion of joy hinted at my heart, slowly pumping, pulsing through my veins. I drew in a breath.

"Are you excited," I asked, knowing full well just how excited she was.

"I can't even wait!" she squealed from her spot, holding her sleeping bag snugly on her lap.

At the stop sign at the end of the street, I peered at her reflection, searching, making sure my six-year-old child was really ready to take this big girl step.

I wasn't entirely sure I was ready for it.

"Are you nervous at all?" My eyes narrowed in question.

She was growing up so fast. And the last few months had been such a blur. I felt as if I'd missed so much. Now, I had the urge to hold on, to cling to her, to relearn my little girl. No doubt, I'd missed much that had shaped her, missed all those little things that had been important to her life.

And as important as the little things were, I had to accept that I'd essentially been absent as Lizzie had to deal and grow accustomed to the trauma she'd been dragged through over the last few months. There was no question it had made a huge impact on her life. Lives had been ripped apart when Lillie's had ended, the hopes and dreams we'd all had crushed.

Sadness thrummed, beat along with that joy I now felt slipping through my veins.

God, these conflicting emotions were overwhelming.

I knew I had to talk to her about it, that I had to *talk*, when I'd done so very little of it since Lillie had been taken from us. Fear held me back, though, fear of opening myself up to the profusion of pain. But for Lizzie, I would, and I'd have to do it soon.

Lizzie's gaze drifted out the window, and she

seemed to ponder my question. She slowly turned back to me. "I don't think so, Mommy. Maybe a little bit. My tummy kind of feels funny, but I think it's in a good way."

A soft smile curved my mouth. She was truly the most amazing child, the depth of her, the way she thought, and the keen way she looked at the world. I studied the road then glanced at her.

"Well, you know my cell phone number, right? If you feel scared at all or just want to talk, you can tell Adriana's mommy that you want to call me, okay?"

"Okay, Mommy."

I turned right onto a narrow neighborhood street and pulled up behind the line of cars parked on either side of the road.

Lizzie was already unbuckled and out the door by the time I went around to her side. She ran up the walkway ahead of me, scrambling up two steps to the ranch-style house, the front lined with lush trees. The front door opened before she had the chance to ring the bell.

Logan stepped out, waving behind him.

"Hey you two." He flashed a wide smile when he noticed us there. He tapped Lizzie's nose. "Are you excited for the party?" he asked her.

"Yes! I'm the most excited in my whole life. Is Kelsey already here?"

"She sure is. Already inside." He inclined his

head toward the door. "You better go catch up with her. She was asking for you."

"Okay." Lizzie raced inside.

I cast a small smile at Logan as I edged toward the entrance. "I'm glad Kelsey will be here tonight. That makes me feel better."

"Me, too. I've been worrying about this all day." He huffed a sigh. "Guess it's time to let them grow up a bit." He ambled down the two steps, turned to the side so he could slide by me. He gestured back to the house with his chin. "It's pure mayhem in there. Prepare yourself. I don't think I've ever seen so much pink in my life."

I laughed and shook my head. "Thanks for the warning."

"Not a problem."

I stepped through the door and into the chaos happening inside. Girls ran, squealing as they howled with laughter. Streamers and balloons hung from what seemed every surface, confetti strewn across the entry table where the gifts were set. I set Lizzie's gift down just as Dana, Adriana's mom, rounded the corner.

Amusement filled her face. "Oh, hi. I thought I saw Lizzie blaze by me about five seconds ago."

I offered an awkward smile as I tried to peer farther into her home. "Are you sure you can handle all these girls tonight?"

"Pfft." She waved a dismissive hand. "They'll be

great. As long as they're having fun, I figure I can handle it."

"Well, you're a brave woman." I hesitated before I cast a cautious glance into the depths of her home. Turning back, I lowered my voice. "I really appreciate you having Lizzie. This is her first sleepover, so just give me a call if she can't sleep or you need me to come pick her up or whatever."

Understanding slipped into her expression. "Of course, Elizabeth. But please don't worry, I think they'll all be fine. We have tons of stuff planned for them, so I figure they'll all pass out by the time bedtime rolls around."

I nodded my thanks then slowly made my way to the end of the hall. The living space was large and open, the kitchen and family room separated only by a large island lined in barstools. Three little girls sat in the middle of the rug, playing dolls, why another handful of them ran wildly from room to room.

Apparently Lizzie was one of them.

"Lizzie," I called as one of the girls flew by, disappearing down another hall. "I'm heading out."

Lizzie came running, appearing out of nowhere. Laughing, she squeezed her arms around me. "I'll miss you!"

I hugged her back, hard and desperate and with all the love I had for my little girl. "You be a good girl, okay?"

She nodded emphatically. "Don't worry, Mommy. I'll be just fine." She almost looked like she was worried for me.

I touched her chin. "Love you."

"Love you, too."

Then she scampered off. I headed back down the entry hall, wished Dana good luck.

The door snapped shut behind me, and I stood in the soft coolness of the setting night. I hugged myself and lifted my face to the sky. For a second, I stilled as one bright star flickered as it slowly seeped into view. Wind gusted in, scattering leaves across my feet.

A soft puff of air escaped through my nose.

I realized no matter what life threw our way, it still sped on.

Shaking my head, I pushed my worries aside, wrapped my sweater a little tighter around myself, and headed down the walkway toward the street.

Startled, I lost my footing when I caught a glimpse of Logan leaning against the front end of my car.

I guess maybe I shouldn't have been all that surprised.

Tucking a sharp shot of air into my lungs, I pushed forward. I came to a stop two feet in front of him.

"You doing okay? I can tell you aren't all that thrilled about this," he said with a concerned tilt of his head.

With longing, I looked back at the house where I knew my daughter played. I pictured the smile that brightened every inch of her precious face, the joy gleaming in her expressive blue eyes, the fun she would surely have. Slowly I turned back to Logan, felt the corners of my eyes crease as I got lost in contemplation.

Logan just leaned back, his hands stuffed in his pockets, completely at ease, casual as he watched me without all the expectations I'd been running from. Another flurry of wind whipped through the air, stirring up the messy chunks of his hair. It flopped in his face. He roughed it back, revealing both of his playful, green eyes.

I wasn't blind. I knew the man was attractive. But that had no bearing on why I liked him, why I liked being in his space.

With Logan, nothing seemed forced, and he stood there watching me without the scrutiny of those who judged, those who wanted responses from me that I didn't want to give.

They'd wanted me to promise them I was okay when I wasn't.

Logan had never once asked me things I didn't want to tell.

Christian's presence slipped just under the surface of my skin. And it hurt and it longed, whispered a call I didn't think I'd ever be able to heed. Because that whisper burned, the memory of that beautiful man ingrained so deeply in my spirit that it now felt like a burden. He'd always be there, a part of me. There was no ridding myself of something so strong. He'd called me today. I'd let it go to voicemail because I just…couldn't.

I managed to push all thoughts of Christian down, tucked them inside where I hid everything else, and focused on Logan.

I offered him a little honesty. "It's hard for me to see her growing up like this." I lifted my shoulders in a confounded shrug. "But then I'm so happy to see her this excited." I paused, chewed at my lip before I fully leveled my eyes on him. "I just want her to be happy."

Simple.

Just like I felt things were with Logan.

"You're a good mom, Liz." His nod was slow and meaningful.

"I wouldn't go that far," I said through a scoff, then shook it off. "Anyway, I better get going." I pointed to my car as if asking him to remove himself from it.

"You have plans tonight?"

"No, not really. I'm just going to get some laundry done."

He laughed and turned his attention to the deepening sky. He was grinning when he looked back at me from the side, his arms crossed up high on his chest. "That's really sad, Liz." Those green eyes gleamed with the tease.

I dropped my gaze to my feet and released a self-conscious chuckle. "Exciting, right?"

"Not so much." He shifted a little. "Listen...I have dinner simmering on the stove. Why don't you come over? We can wallow in our little girls growing up together."

I took a single step back. "I don't think that's a good idea."

"Oh, come on, how could it be a bad idea? I have dinner and wine. There aren't many things better than that."

Over my shoulder, I gazed at the house. Lights glowed bright from all the windows. So much life was happening inside.

I wanted to...I wanted to do something different than spending another night alone at my house. Each night this week it had just gotten harder to bear.

Still, something held me back, a hesitation that hammered in my heart.

Something that felt inherently wrong.

"Why don't you drive back to your house," he continued, "leave your car, and you can ride over with me. That way you can have a glass of wine, relax, enjoy yourself a little."

I wavered, my head tipped to the side as I tried to decipher his intention. I wasn't a fool. I saw it in his eyes, read it in his actions, the way he stayed just a little too long and talked just a little too much, the attraction that was there. I knew he wanted something to develop between us.

Could it?

Now?

In time?

I just didn't know.

As if he read every last one of my thoughts, he shook his head and laughed. "God, Liz, you worry too much. It's just dinner." His toothy grin was wide and without a trace of strain. Nonchalant.

But was it? Was that what he really intended it to be? Is that what I intended? Because I was lonely. I could admit it now. I *missed* something, but I couldn't exactly pinpoint what it was that I was missing.

I finally conceded, because in the end, I couldn't stand the thought of walking into the emptiness of my house. "That sounds nice, I guess."

His smile widened even more. "You guess, huh?" He splayed his hand over his heart. "You wound me, Liz."

A sputter of laughter tripped from my mouth. I couldn't help it.

Then he stood and straightened himself out. "Let me grab my car, and I'll follow you over."

"Okay," I agreed.

By the time I sat down in my car, I was shaking.

I fumbled to get the key into the ignition. I glanced to where Logan was parked on the opposite side of the street, facing me.

What was I doing?

God, I had no idea.

I had no idea what I felt or what I needed.

Starting my car, I flipped a U-turn and headed back toward my house. Headlights gleamed in my rearview mirror, a constant reminder that a different man than the one I'd thought I'd spend my life with tailed me, followed with unknown intentions. I had a feeling tonight he would make them clear.

I pulled into my garage and cut the engine. My heart skittered, and I couldn't tell if it was a pleasant or unwelcomed sensation.

I will try.

I realized this was part of it, moving on, *living*. Hiding away was no longer an option.

With the keypad, I tapped in the code and closed the garage. I started toward Logan's car. I couldn't help but grin when he ran around to the passenger door and opened it, dipped himself in an exaggerated bow.

"Ma'am."

I laughed, and it felt good.

seventeen

Night steadily swallowed the heavens, a blanket of

darkness strewn across the sky. Under it, I felt caged. Edgy. My headlights splayed across the road, the cabin dim, the high whine of my engine nipping at my ears as I sped the short distance from Matthew and Natalie's house to Elizabeth's.

I didn't matter if she was there or not. I'd wait.

It was time.

Time to bring all this shit out into the open. Grief fisted my chest, thrashed at my ribs as words that needed to be said, hurt that needed to be confessed.

I knew Elizabeth had plenty of her own that needed to be shed.

Impatience bounced my knee as I stopped at a red stoplight. Thirty seconds passed like an eternity. Finally, it changed, and I accelerated, surging through the thick evening traffic. I merged into the turn lane and made a left onto the narrow road. Trees rose up on every side. Lights glowed their warmth from the windows where families ate dinner within the walls of their houses, where they played and laughed and loved. This neighborhood had always felt that way. Safe. Peaceful. Like home.

Twice I'd driven this road when I had been certain my heart would pound right out of my chest. Falter. Cease to sustain my life.

The first was the day I'd come here not even knowing my daughter's name, not knowing the circumstances of their lives or the pain my decisions had brought them. I'd been unprepared then for what I had found. Elizabeth living alone, without love, solely supporting the daughter I'd abandoned.

That day had broken me, thrusting all my regrets and mistakes to the forefront. I'd finally had to accept the true consequences of the appalling choices I had made. But in that day, I'd still found light. A purpose. Hope. An inundating swell of devotion had pulsed steadily through my veins as I watched the two girls I loved with all of me embracing each other at the end of Elizabeth's drive. That moment in time marked the day when I made the decision to take my family back. When I'd stood up, taken on the responsibility that had always been mine. When I finally knew I had to make it *right*.

The second was today.

As I inched my car down the quieted hush of the neighborhood street, my heart rate ratcheted high. It thundered to a roar in my ears and sloshed blood through my veins, pushed and pressed and tugged.

I approached slowly.

Three long blinks shielded my disbelieving eyes, the air punched from my lungs. I didn't want to see. Still, I couldn't help but look, as if I were drawn to the slaughter.

Like I'd done that first day, I pulled to the curb on the opposite side of the road and concealed myself behind the cover of another car.

But unlike then, today was without that hope. Without the bright flash of light that had been injected into my weary life.

Today, there was just anger and pain and anguish that shocked across my skin.

A tremor shook me, rattled to my bones, and I struggled to draw in a breath of stifled air. But there was none to be found.

Part of me was screaming at myself to get up, to get out, to stop the ruin playing out in slow motion in front of me.

The other was frozen, pinned to that wall that seemed impossible to break free from.

Pain slammed me, sliced me in two, severing the few frayed threads that were holding my sanity together. That one that had held the last piece of my heart.

My vision blurred.

That asshole was here, standing at the passenger door of his car, holding it open as if he were some kind of fucked up knight in shining armor.

Playing a bastard's game where he won and I lost my family.

Elizabeth rushed down her driveway to where he waited for her on the street.

And she laughed.

She fucking laughed and got in his car.

He slammed her door shut and ran around to the driver's side. Brake lights flashed as he shifted the car into drive. Easing back onto the road, he headed in the opposite direction than the way we normally came in from the main street.

He was taking her to his house.

I knew it.

Motherfucker.

Images assaulted my mind. My fingers constricted around the steering wheel, my knuckles white. Furiously I blinked, struggling to see through the madness that clouded my sight. Anger singed my blood, pounded faster and harder and consumed every inch of my being.

Had they been doing this? Sneaking away? When Lizzie was at my house, was she with him?

Unable to stop myself, I followed, knowing there was no other choice. I fought to grasp onto one rational thought as I trailed them at a distance. Taillights burned a path ahead of me, like a beacon. Or maybe a warning flare.

Because the end result of this night remained unknown.

But it would have a result.

And it very well may be the end.

eighteen

Logan pulled his car into his garage.

I spent the entire ride over fretting, questioning the decision I made to come here.

And the ride had been short.

That didn't mean a million thoughts hadn't spun through my overactive mind, confusion and contention and doubt.

Inside, I'd warred.

I guess what scared me most was I really didn't know myself anymore. Didn't recognize the woman sitting in this seat who was going to another man's house.

What was I doing here?

Was I fool? Because any wise woman would know a man didn't take her back to his house to talk. Logan wasn't looking for a friend. He was looking for something I wasn't sure I was ready to give.

He reached up to the visor and pushed the button to lower the garage door. The loud chain ran, spinning on wheels as the door slowly settled to the concrete floor. In it came a silence, a claustrophobic sense that made me want to jump out of my skin.

Logan patted me on the thigh. A flirty smile curved his upper lip as he looked over at me. "Come on, Liz, let's get some dinner, I'm starving."

We climbed out. He spun his keyring on his index finger as he walked toward the door that led into the house. He stepped aside as he held it open for me. "After you."

Dropping my head, I acquiesced, ignoring the warning blaring within my head.

I promised I would try, and I knew I had to see this through.

Stepping inside, I found myself standing within cluttered piles of dirty clothes that sat in heaps on the floor in the small, enclosed laundry room that led into his house.

Self-conscious laughter seeped into the small room from behind. "You'll have to excuse the mess. I wasn't expecting company, although I have to admit, I'm really happy to have it."

From over my shoulder, I forced a smile as I sidestepped around the mess. "Don't worry about it. You should see mine. I think I have enough laundry to keep me busy for the next three months."

He placed a warm hand on the small of my back as he guided me, bringing us out into a short hall. "To the left," he instructed, prodding me forward with the heat of his hand.

A sharp breath left me. I wasn't sure I liked it.

I hurried ahead.

He dropped his hand and began flipping on lights as we headed toward the front of his house. We stepped into the family room and he wove around to the far wall to flip on the light.

His home was much like mine, modest, the tiny rooms stuffed with so many mementos that it was cluttered in the most comfortable way.

I'd been here several times, dropping Lizzie off or picking her up, and of course I'd been inside during the barbeque last weekend. But being here, alone with him, it felt entirely different. Claustrophobic. Confined.

From where he stood on the other side of the couch, he smiled at me. "It's quiet in here without the girls running around, isn't it?"

I guess maybe he felt it, too.

"Yeah," I said. Too quiet.

I fixed a plaintive smile on him, not really knowing what I was doing here, wondering why I stayed.

God, I was so messed up. Wrecked. I realized it a long time ago as I'd been lost in my misery. As my mind had begun to clear, I'd accepted it. Maybe even understood it.

My eyes narrowed as I studied Logan from across the room, and I wondered if he saw it in me. Did he know how broken I was? Did he know I was a mess? That most mornings, I could barely get out of bed?

Did he know I ached for a little girl I would never again hold? Did he know she haunted me? Did he know I'd never let her go?

What was he after? A fast fix? A fuck? A vulnerable woman who lacked common sense because she was blinded by pain?

Maybe I could give him that.

Maybe for a few minutes, it would cover it, the hurt and the sorrow and the cruelty of this world.

Or did he see something different in me? A companion. Someone who understood. A parent with similar circumstances, someone who was alone, one who was spinning away her days until something finally made sense.

Would it ever?

Because nothing made sense now. Not being here. Not looking at him. Not the confusion wreaking havoc on my emotions.

Maybe the most important question was the one that burned bright, the one that nagged, the one that promised Christian could never be scraped from my consciousness. No blade was sharp enough. No cut could ever go deep enough.

Did Logan know he could never compare?

Standing here, in his house, watching him from across the span of this tiny room, this nonchalant man with the insipid smile, I knew. I knew the mark Christian had made. It was profound. Permanent.

And it ached.

Logan tipped his head toward the kitchen archway. "I'd better check on the sauce. I'm making spaghetti, if that's okay?"

Delirious laughter threatened, but I bit it back, held it in. Of course he was. The past seemed to be mocking me. Maybe such a simple dinner was common, but it didn't matter. It still belonged to Christian and me. How many times had we stood in my tiny kitchen after we had reconciled, Christian's arms wrapped around my expanding waist, his face buried in my hair as he sought out my neck, kissing me there. I could almost hear his voice in my ear. *Are you making my favorite? Smells so good, baby. You spoil me. Let me finish.*

I drew in a staggered breath.

"Yeah, that's great," I forced out.

Concern deepened the lines on Logan's face. He cocked his head. "You sure? Because if you don't like spaghetti, I can dump it and start over. Better yet, we could go out to dinner."

I realized then how clueless he was. He didn't know me. The man had no idea what hurt me and what touched me. What would turn me on and what would shut me down.

I shook a little.

Was that what I wanted?

To start fresh?

To leave behind all the memories that would forever haunt me? Did I want to forget the ones that had meant most to me in favor of shunning the hurt?

It seemed the only option, because I didn't know how else to stand up under the pain.

A soft sound sifted from me, and I shook my head. "No, honestly, I love spaghetti. It's one of my favorites."

His concern washed to confusion. "All right, then." He turned and passed through the archway.

I followed him into his kitchen. It was small, but updated. The black granite countertops gleamed with specks of silver, black appliances to match, the dark wood cabinets warm.

I tried to relax within it. It was one of the coziest kitchens I'd ever been in, a lot like those we'd seen in the homes Christian and I had been looking to buy.

Logan went straight for the large skillet simmering on the stove. He lifted the lid. Steam curled as it rose, and he leaned over it to take in the aroma.

"Mmm…smells good." He opened a drawer beside him, rustled around inside, and produced a spoon. He dipped it into the thick, red sauce. "Here…taste."

He held it out for me, an offering.

Cautiously I approached, this timorous edge to my movements. My lips parted as I leaned forward to accept the spoon. He cupped his hand under it as he lifted it to my mouth and slipped it inside.

It was hot, burned my tongue, the savory sauce strong. I swallowed and pulled away, our faces too close as eager green eyes studied me. "It's delicious," I mumbled.

His brow shot up. "Yeah?"

"Honest."

He smiled and raked his teeth on his bottom lip. Then he laughed, the sound cocky and sure, breaking the band of tension that had stretched us tight.

"Well, that's a damn good thing, Liz, because it's my mom's special recipe. Not liking my momma's food is a deal breaker."

I shook my head, looked at my feet as I laughed away my discomfort, forcing myself to relax. I cautioned a glance up at him beneath the heavy drop of bangs that had fallen across my forehead. "Deal breaker, huh? And just what kind of deal am I agreeing to?"

He chuckled and scratched at the fine stubble on his chin. "Well, I guess that depends on how much you can handle."

Everything slowed, that thick cord of tension making a resurgence, sucking the air from this little room.

I stepped back, and he turned his head down and to the side, his hands on his hips. He grinned when he looked back up, quick to change the subject.

"Would you like a glass of wine?"

He busied himself searching through the small wine rack tucked at the end of the counter, pulled a bottle out and held it up. "Red okay?"

I forced myself into a detached demeanor, told myself again that I had to try. "Yeah, that sounds nice."

Opening an overhead cabinet, he produced two wine glasses. His lips pressed into a thin line as he worked the cork free on the bottle and pulled it loose. He filled the glasses halfway, passed one to me. He glimmered a smile.

He held out his glass. "To our little girls who are growing up."

Lillie struck me like an errant bolt of lightning. My child who would never grow. I squeezed my eyes against it, against his words, and focused instead on my Lizzie. Reluctantly I clinked my glass his.

"To our little girls."

We both took a deep pull of our wine.

He lifted his glass, tipped it just to the side, gesturing toward the stove. "I'm just going to get the water started for the pasta. Then we can sit down and relax a bit before we eat."

"Is there anything I can do to help?"

"Nah, relax. Enjoy yourself."

He got the water ready to boil and turned back to me. His mouth curved in clear perusal, as if he liked what he saw. He took five steps toward me, each one cutting off a little more of the airflow that fed my deflated lungs.

He held out his hand. "Come here."

I let my hand slip into his. It was a test, to see how it would feel.

And maybe it was wrong, all of it, his skin against mine, my surrender. But I wanted to try.

I needed to try, because I was so tired of feeling dead. I wanted to *feel*. But when I gave into feeling, I couldn't bear for it to hurt. I'd hurt for too long. For just one night, I wanted to feel good.

Not the way I knew Christian's touch would burn me, the way it blessed me and bled me, the way he would singe me as his fingers traced my skin, the way he would sear me with his kiss.

I couldn't handle anything so intense.

Something knotted at the center of my chest, something heavy, something vital.

I breathed around it.

Logan led me back into the family room and set his glass down on the end table. He swept his free hand across a rumpled blanket and dog-eared parenting book abandoned in the middle of the couch, pushing them aside.

A grin flitted at one corner of his mouth. "I warned you my place was a mess."

An awkward huff worked its way free of my tightened throat, me standing there with my hand wound with a man's that I didn't even know.

And again, I was asking myself what I was doing, just what it was I hoped to achieve.

I will try.

He squeezed my hand and pulled me in front of him, guiding me to sit on the smooth leather of his dark brown couch. I sat perched at the edge, ill at ease, a subtle rock of my being as I fought against the urge to run, the desire to stay.

I want to feel something good.

Picking up his glass, Logan sat down beside me. He talked about the girl's teacher, the school, laughed about how stressful it was being in charge of the group of six girls he'd chaperoned on the field trip last week.

I engaged him the best I could, laughed in all the right places because I had nothing to add. I'd been absent the entirety of this school year, absent from our lives.

I will try.

We sipped at our wine, talked about nothing.

Logan set his empty wine glass aside and moved to sit on the large square ottoman in front of me. He took my hand in both of his. "I'm really glad you're here, Liz."

I blinked. Emotions lashed within me. Volatile. Violent. "I'm glad I'm here, too."

He seemed to choke over his laughter. It seemed so out of character for this man, but then I had to admit, I really didn't know him at all. He was my daughter's friend's father. Nothing more. And here I sat with my hand burning between the heat of both of his.

Pulling back, he splayed what seemed to be a nervous hand through his messy hair. For a moment, he looked away, then turned his attention back to me. All the casualness I'd come to expect from him evaporated, severity taking its place.

"I've wanted to do something since the first time I saw you." His hands tightened on mine as he inclined his head, searching, seeking permission.

I chewed at my lip, that disquiet from before bold, sinking aggressive fingers into my spirit.

"See...that...right there. It drives me insane, Liz. That mouth."

He took my face in his hands, his hold strong, fierce as he stared at me with zealous eyes. When he leaned forward, I didn't stop him. I let him. I wanted to feel.

Could he? Could he cover the pain? Expose something in me that was good?

His lips brushed mine, a breath, a brush, insignificance.

Still, it stole what little air I could find.

A whimper passed my parted lips. Something he seemed to mistake as desire. He pressed harder, his firm lips searching mine. He groaned and jerked back, his hold unfailing as his attention jumped all over my face. He gripped me tight.

"God, I've wanted to do that for so long. Did you know that, Liz? That I've been wanting to taste you? And you taste amazing."

He lifted his chin, inclined his head as he dipped, and he searched me again, his mouth powerful as it explored mine. Then he deepened it, his tongue making a rough pass across my trembling bottom lip.

A jagged gasp ripped through my constricted airways. Tore through me with an avenging fury.

This kiss.

It was shattering.

Shred me to pieces, splintered as it fell, demolished the walls I'd erected around me.

This kiss came with a ruthless force.

It cut me open.

Splayed the wounds wide. They bled, surged, flooded me in everything I'd never wanted to feel again.

My mind shot to Christian, and suddenly I was back on my family room couch. And I could feel him, feel him holding me.

"I love you, Christian. Always. There is nothing that could make me stop loving you. Nothing that could make me stop needing you. You are my start and you are my finish, the one who's going to be there for everything in between."

And I *felt*…but I felt everything I'd been so desperately trying to shut out.

It hurt.

Oh my God, it hurt so bad.

I fisted Logan's shirt, needing something to hang on to.

He edged forward, his hand coming to the back of my neck as he kissed me.

I was drowning.

Incredulous laughter shot from my mouth in a contemptuous scoff. "What do you mean, how can I say that?" I pushed up on my knees. "I was the one who carried her, Christian." I jabbed my finger to my chest. "I was the one who loved her and cared for her. She died inside of me and I had to give birth to her." I lifted my chin. *"So yeah, I can say that...you have no idea what I'm feeling. None."*

His entire face twisted in contention. "You think she meant less to me than to you? You think my heart isn't broken over this?"

"You wouldn't even touch her." It dripped from my mouth as a sneer.

Anger bled free.

Overbearing.

Brutal.

Destructive.

A sob tore up my throat.

Logan jerked back, holding my face at a distance as if to hold back the chaos raging though me, panic firing in his green eyes. "Oh my God, Liz, I'm so sorry...I didn't mean..."

We both jumped when we heard the crash at the front door. Our attention whipped around just as Christian barreled in. He seemed to get knocked to a standstill when he saw Logan and me twisted up together.

Violence trembled from his seething bones, his face pinched in pain as he cast his devastation on me.

Logan jumped to his feet, his body a barricade as he stepped in front of me. His voice dropped in slow disbelief. "Are you out of your fucking mind?"

Protective aggression curled through his muscles as he took a stance in front of me. Shielding me.

That was impossible. There was no defense. Nothing that could defend me from the force of Christian.

I stared up at the man, the one who inhabited every significant memory of my life, the pain and the joy, the love and the ecstasy, the misery and the torment.

And anger.

It was glaring. Overwhelming.

I was *so* angry.

Blue eyes blazed at me with disgust, destroyed, spearing me to the couch.

Pain sliced through me, the sharpest knife driven into the pit of my stomach.

And I hurt.

How was it possible to hate a man I loved so much?

nineteen

*E*lizabeth and I had been through so much.

Indescribable bliss and devastating sorrow.

Our love ran so deep, and yet, it seemed our wounds ran deeper.

Some of those wounds had seemed unbearable, inflictions impossible to recover from.

No doubt one came with the regrets of the greatest mistake I'd ever made, the day Elizabeth had been forced to choose between me and Lizzie before she was even born, the day I'd sent her away to live life on her own, scared and alone.

Another had been the day Lillie was taken from us. Our hearts had ruptured when she was ripped from our lives.

I once believed the other had been the day I'd walked out of Elizabeth's house little more than three months ago. I couldn't imagine hurting any worse than that moment, when I'd snapped the door shut to block out the overwhelming sorrow of the woman I loved, a wall put up between us because neither of us knew how to deal with the excruciating pain.

But that moment didn't come close to the devastation that hit me now.

Elizabeth balanced just on the edge of his couch, one leg canted off to the side as if she were getting ready to slip onto the asshole's lap. Those fingers I knew so well were tangled in his shirt while he held her perfect face between his filthy hands.

Malice curled my hands into fists as I took in the brutality happening ten feet away from me.

He was kissing her.

He was fucking kissing her and touching her.

And the bastard had the nerve to do it while she still wore my ring.

Her head spun in my direction, breaking their connection. Shock widened her brown eyes as she gaped at me from across the short span of the room. Still, it felt like I'd never been further from her than I was now. The distance so great. An impenetrable expanse.

Logan jumped to his feet, and the asshole moved to stand in front of her. Misplaced aggression coiled his muscles. As if I were in the wrong. As if he thought it his job to keep her from me. That was his intention. I knew it. Possessiveness radiated from his posture, as if he had some kind of claim on her.

But he had none.

She was mine, and she was always going to be.

Even through the barrier Logan tried to forge between us, her wary gaze held mine. A storm raged in her expression, tightened in shock, taut in anger, flashed with distinct relief and adoration. I didn't know if Elizabeth recognized she still held it for me.

The asshole's voice rang somewhere in my mind. "Are you out of your fucking mind?"

My attention snapped up to meet his sneer.

Yes, I was most definitely out of my fucking mind.

How could she do this to me?

I said it aloud, the trauma flowing free. "How could you do this, Elizabeth?" It was an accusation, a rush of emotion squeezed from within. I looked at her with disbelieving eyes, my head slowly shaking as the pain tore through me. "How could you?"

Tears slipped down her face, her lips quivering.

And I knew she had been crying, even before I broke through the door. Like maybe she felt it, too, the chaos that had spun me into a complete fucking frenzy as I pounded the sidewalk outside the bastard's house for the last fifteen minutes. When I couldn't take it any longer, I'd tried to peer through the drapes of his window, the two silhouettes obscured, though I'd seen them leaning, pressing, moving.

There was no more standing aside.

I was taking her back.

Logan inched a little farther in front of her. He cocked his head to the side as he narrowed his eyes. "Get the fuck out of my house."

My laughter was ragged, verging on hysterical.

Because there was no sanity in this situation.

"I'm not going anywhere without her." I spit the words at him.

Elizabeth whimpered, grasping at the collar of her shirt as she scrambled back on his couch, climbing to her feet on unsteady legs.

I could see the line of her, her face blocked from view, her body shaking as she fumbled a few steps back. And it almost felt like relief when she came around and stood in the small open area behind the couch. Her face was downturned, and she wavered in indecision.

I made it for her.

"Go get in my car, Elizabeth." The command slid out low.

A cry erupted from her, as if she were in physical pain. I knew she was.

Logan rushed around the other side of the couch, as if to shield her, as if he knew anything about the woman crumbling in the middle of his room. "She isn't going anywhere with you." He extended his arm back to keep her at bay. "Baby, stay back," came as a quiet assault from his mouth, as if he were sharing some kind of private conversation with her, telling her without words that she didn't have to be afraid of me.

Baby.

He called her baby.

Hostility rolled from me in waves as a sweep of possessiveness broke, taking over every cell in my body.

When he took a single step toward me, I charged him. My shoulder collided with his chest.

A horrified scream rose up from Elizabeth, blended with the cries she couldn't seem to contain. They fed the agitation, the madness that left me unhinged. Because without Elizabeth, I was in pieces. Shattered.

Caught off guard, Logan fumbled backward before he regained his balance. On his toes, he bounced in aggression.

"You are fucking crazy," wheezed from his

lungs. He rushed in, swung wide as he aimed for my face. The punch missed as I ducked my head.

My arm cocked back, insanity flooding from me unlike anything I'd ever known. All I knew was I wouldn't let him have her. I wouldn't, and I couldn't fucking stand the thought, knowing that the two of them had been together.

Was she sleeping with him? Had she been curled up with him in his bed?

Blinded with fury, I slammed my fist into the underside of his jaw. His head rocked back.

A guttural groan roared from his throat.

Her undying presence nipped at my soul, teased and taunted as I bore down on this asshole who for even a second thought she could somehow be his.

I hit him again, the strike landing on his cheek.

He stumbled back, his own fury mounting a resistance as he surged forward.

Elizabeth screamed.

My attention darted to her, to the one I wasn't sure I knew any longer.

Sadness poured from her as she witnessed me coming unglued.

Unprepared, distracted by her, his fist connected with my nose. Pain exploded, splitting my vision.

Blood gushed, and I saw red.

I lost it, losing myself in the pent-up rage that I'd harbored for so long. I unleashed it on him, the anger for her, the anger for me, the anger at the injustice of this fucked up world.

Her desperate voice hit my ears. "Christian, please, stop."

I stumbled back, aggression still curling through my senses as I glared down at the piece of shit who was trying to steal her from me.

I swiped the back of my hand beneath my nose and across my mouth. Blood smeared. Sniffing, I turned my attention to Elizabeth. She was crying, lost, just as fucking lost as me.

"Go get in my car, Elizabeth." It was hard, harsh with the anger. I realized most of it was directed at her.

She vacillated, shifting, so obviously drawn to the door and drawn to this place where she hid, where she hid behind lies and pretended she didn't have to face what we'd gone through. Her unsteady gaze met with the intensity of mine.

"Go," I said.

The brown of her eyes flamed and dimmed, a roil of confusion, harboring a disturbance unlike anything I'd ever witnessed, a disturbance as severe as the one boiling inside of me.

Anger and regret.

Revulsion.

Pain, prominent and suffocating.

Underneath it all was the love that would ever let us go.

She dropped her gaze and shuffled around me, quietly slipping out the door.

I stared at Logan who was trying to pick himself up off the floor, my entire body rocking with hatred. Blood dripped from my nose. Harshly, I wiped it with the back of my hand.

"Stay away from her. Do you understand me? This is *my* family. Did you see that ring on her finger? Do you think this is a game? That woman belongs to me. She always has and she always will. Don't think for a second you can take her from me. She will love me until the day she dies."

I'd told a million lies in my lifetime.

That statement was one I knew as the truth.

"Fuck you," he sneered, roughing the heel of his hand across his bleeding face.

Derisive laughter flooded from me. I backed up, lifting an accusatory finger at him as he straightened. "I'm not joking. Stay away from her. You don't know her...not for a second...don't pretend like you do."

Then I turned and ran out the door I'd barreled through not five minutes before.

Maybe I'd fucked up and maybe there'd be consequences to pay, my actions lawless as I'd lost myself in my rage. But that mattered none. I'd made a promise to fight for her, and I'd pay whatever cost.

She was worth everything.

Night had completely taken hold, the darkness thick, a blanket of clouds squatting heavily over the city. My silver Audi sat at the curb. The tinted windows concealed Elizabeth waiting inside.

I fought against the anger still burning through my blood, fought against the image of the two of them on his couch. I was sure I'd never be able to purge it from my mind. It blinded me. Scrubbing my palm over my face, I opened the door. The overhead light glowed to life, illuminating Elizabeth in the passenger seat. With her head downcast, she twisted her fingers in knots on her lap.

I sat down, started my car, and put it in drive. Tension stretched between us, the tightest band, something explosive threatening to snap. Anger and fury and unanswered questions bounced between us as I seethed in the silence.

I glanced at her, my lip curling as I swiped the residual of blood from my lip. She didn't look at me. She just slowly rocked and cried, silent tears gleaming in the street lights that flashed through the windows.

God, I loved her so much. I wanted to hold her, tell her it was going to be okay in the same second I wanted to lash out at her.

It took me all of thirty seconds to get back to her house.

I pulled into the drive and cut the engine. It

ticked and hummed. We just sat there, me looking ahead, Elizabeth staring at her hands. The air was so thick, and I could almost hear the heavy thud of her heart. Nausea swirled in my raw stomach.

How would we ever get past this?

With her head down, Elizabeth fumbled blindly with the handle, a sob escaping her as she clambered from my car.

Climbing out, I trailed her up the walkway toward the front door. In the stagnant silence that twisted us tight, there was no room to breathe.

The air was thick, heavy, dense as I hovered right behind her while she fumbled to produce her keys. She trembled as she slid it into the lock and let us into the house that was supposed to be our home.

The door swung open.

She stepped inside, stopping in the entry with her back to me.

Quietly I latched the door behind us, and I edged forward, my chest an inch from her back. A single light burned from deep within the kitchen. It cast a faint glow into the dim-lit room. The walls enclosed around us, a stir of anger and a rush of need. I could smell her, her hair brushing against me as she inhaled, her body palpitating with the ragged breath.

"Did you fuck him?" The words dropped from me in a slow accusation. It was laced with all the hurt of finding the two of them together.

I sensed every one of her muscles tighten, the slow sway of her body as she shook her head.

"No."

It was a whisper, enough to weaken my knees with the rush of relief, still stoked the fury for what she had given into.

My fingers weaved through her hair, and I barely tugged her back, her jaw lifting as I brought my mouth to her ear. "Is that what you want, Elizabeth? Someone else to touch you?"

A tortured whimper escaped her throat. "No."

Slowly I turned her around and pushed her up against the wall beside the door. Her back hit it with a thud. A whine rose from deep within her, escaped as agony into the room, something akin to the torture eating me alive. Brown eyes flashed to mine, and she lifted her chin, rigid, this broken girl who looked at me with bitterness and need.

I fluttered my fingertips down the slope of her neck. Every ounce of the pain she'd caused me squeezed into the words that I forced from my mouth.

"Tell me you don't love me anymore."

She clenched her jaw.

I erased all the space separating us, flattening myself to her as she shrank against the wall. Still she said nothing.

I curved my fingers around her neck, my thumb

pressing under her jaw as I forced her to look at me. "Tell me you don't love me anymore, Elizabeth."

A strangled sob broke loose from her, bounced around the strained tension of the tiny room.

I gripped her face between my hands. My mouth descended on hers. Her lips were chapped, pouty and full, all wrong and perfectly right. And I wanted to erase it, expunge the asshole from her lips, delete the past.

Elizabeth kissed me desperately as she clawed at my neck, fingers sinking deep, cutting me more as she struggled to bring me closer.

More fucking pain.

"Tell me...tell me you don't love me."

Her hands fisted in my shirt, and she hit me, pounded my chest. "I hate you," she whispered hard, tortured, her fingers curling into the skin at my jaw.

She kissed me harder as she locked her fingers in my hair.

We lit. A frenzy took us over as we gripped and clutched, as she bit and hit and begged.

The anger we'd left unresolved the day I'd walked out pulsed between us, a force that neither of us could stop.

My kiss was demanding, urgent as I consumed her. Hers, desperate.

I ripped her shirt over her head. "Tell me to

stop," I pleaded. My body strained, clashed with the fury of what she'd done, the pain she'd caused, collided with the grief that devoured Elizabeth.

Another sob.

My arm wound around her waist, and I dropped us to our knees and laid her on the floor. Her chest heaved as tears streamed.

She tore at my skin, claimed it again. "I hate you."

I caged her, raked my nose up her jaw and to her ear. "Tell me you don't love me." It came harsh, acute and severe.

She slapped me across the face, before her fingers locked on the back of my neck, pulling me back to her. She forced her mouth against mine, and I lost it, kissed her and kissed her, tore at her clothes, desperate to feel her against me. I needed her. Oh my God, I needed her. And yet she'd hurt me, cut me so deep, I didn't know how to see, had no clue how to make sense of any of this except I refused to let her go.

My pleas changed as I ripped the panties from her body and fumbled with the button on my jeans. "Tell me to stop, Elizabeth. Tell me to stop," I ordered as I shed my clothes.

"Don't you dare stop." She raked her nails down my back, drawing blood, her body begging for mine. "Don't ever stop."

I slammed into her.

I cried out in pleasured relief.

And I fucked her. I fucked her and fucked her, because I was angry. Angry she'd let that bastard kiss her. Angry that I had let her slip away. Angry that Lillie had been stolen from us. Angry that I hadn't been strong enough to hold her together when she'd fallen apart.

And she was crying, crying as I claimed her. Marked her. Took back what was mine. I felt her convulse around me, her body gripping my cock as she came. Still, she cried, she cried and raged and pounded out all of her pain against my chest.

Her name crashed from my mouth as I poured into her. It was agony. It was ecstasy. I collapsed on her, my chest to hers.

Elizabeth went limp below me, but she was clinging, weeping against my skin. "Why didn't you love her?" Fingertips bored deep, cutting into my spirit. "Why didn't you love her?" she asked on a muted sob.

I held my weight on my forearms as I sank my nose in the warmth of her neck. I ran my fingers through her hair, kissed her jaw, whispered at her ear. "I loved her, Elizabeth…so much…I loved her so much." It was low, ragged, a promise for the one who would forever live in our hearts.

A little girl who had touched our lives.

A little girl who had torn it apart.

A trauma we could not sustain.

And she wept. Elizabeth wept, and I just held her.

Finally I got to my knees, gathered this broken woman in my arms, and climbed to my feet. Elizabeth wrapped her arms around my neck. I hugged her to me, kissed her forehead as I carried her upstairs.

"I love you, Christian." I felt her words more than heard them.

"I know," I whispered tenderly at her skin, all of mine held in the simple acceptance of what she had said.

With my foot, I nudged the bedroom door open. Crossing the room, I gently settled her in the middle of the bed. Elizabeth looked up at me with all the torment she had been unwilling to show, her eyes open wide, the darkness in the depths revealing how deep her pain really went.

My movements were measured as I climbed down beside her. I tugged her twisted sheets over us as I turned to my side and pulled her into my arms.

There was no resistance. Her arms were crossed between us as I held her whole, my hand at the back of her head while she cried out months of misery into my chest.

I held her, supported her the way I should have, even when she'd pushed me away.

"I'm so sorry," I finally managed to murmur. I

ran my fingers through the length of her hair. "I'm so sorry for everything. For everything."

She curled her hand into the skin at my chest, fingers anchoring deep. "Don't leave me."

Exhaling, I somehow managed to pull her a little closer. I would never let her go.

"Never, Elizabeth. I wasn't going anywhere. I was just waiting for you to come back to me."

In all of this, that had been my greatest mistake, my biggest failure. Leaving her alone when she needed me most.

Another sob echoed from her mouth. "It hurts," she whimpered.

"I know, baby, I know."

She choked over the emotion in her chest. I held her tighter. Never again would I allow enough space for a wedge to be driven between us. I'd never sit silent. I'd no longer wait.

I whispered into her hair softly, "It is time, Elizabeth."

I said those three words again, the ones that had continually been our ruin. I wasn't scared saying them now. "It's time to talk about it. To talk about her. Talk about us. You have to *tell* me what you're feeling."

Elizabeth burrowed deeper, her tears wet on my flesh. "It hurts," she said again.

"I know. It hurts me, too, but we *have* to."

Hiding only ruined us, destroyed what we had.

Slowly, she lifted her face to me, and I stared down at the woman I loved, silently encouraging her to open up to me.

She swallowed hard before her face pinched and a rush of tears streamed from the creases of her eyes. "That day, Christian." Her lids closed as if she were trying to block the memory, or maybe she was finally allowing it in. The words were rough, pained. "Going through labor...it was torture." She glanced at me, searching for understanding. "It felt like I was rejecting her when all I wanted to do was hang onto her. But then they brought her to me..."

She wet her lips, her attention darting away before it flitted back to search my face, agony set in every line. "All that time when I was holding her, I kept begging her to breathe. She felt so whole in my arms that I kept thinking she *had* to. She just had to take a breath, and everything would be okay."

I could feel her panic, the pain as it rolled through her, as it tightened in her throat and hammered furiously in her chest.

I wanted to fix it, to fix her, to shield her, but I knew we had to face it, and facing it was going to hurt. All of it, the pain in what we'd lost and the disaster we'd created in its wake.

My arms constricted around her body. She felt so frail in my arms, so delicate. Shudders wracked through her as she trembled in my hold.

"Baby, I know it hurts, but you have to *tell* me. We're never going to get past this if we don't talk to each other."

Her fingers burrowed into my skin, as if seeking an anchor. Her words came with a crush of sorrow, unbearable as she once again broke down.

"When they took her away, it was like reality finally hit me, and that was the moment when I realized she never would, Christian. My little girl was never going to breathe, and when they walked out the door with her, she took my ability to breathe with her."

And I was there again, with her, seeing it through her eyes. And God, it was fucking devastating.

"I felt like I was suffocating, Christian, and I thought I was going to die. And you...you were the one who made me do it. You were the one who told me it was time." She pinched her eyes closed. "God, this is so hard to talk about, I've kept it inside for so long."

"Baby...take your time."

She took a deep breath, blinking as she slowly shook her head. "I know now how crazy that was, Christian. I blamed you for something you couldn't control, but it felt like you were *against* me, like you weren't fighting for her the way I was. I hated you for it."

Hearing her say it again punched me in the gut. I knew she had, but I also knew it'd come from trauma, from shock, that she'd been lost to skewed emotions because she didn't know how to deal with the loss.

I cupped her cheek, my thumb making a pass over the apple of her cheek. "It's okay, Elizabeth. Just tell me...I want to hear it. I need to hear it so I can understand."

She looked up at me through watery eyes, her expression intense.

"You didn't hold her." Her mouth quivered as she said it. She glanced away, then brought her attention back to me. "I know what I said to you was *selfish* because I know you loved her. But that hurt me, and it just added to the anger I felt toward you. Every time I saw you, the pain almost knocked me from my feet. I couldn't feel anything else but the pain and the hurt and the hate. And the pain is still there," she emphasized, "I need you to know that I'm scared and I'm confused lying here with you, but the pain is not obscuring what I really feel for you anymore."

Hope wound into her voice. "The last few weeks, I've been feeling it, little flashes of something that felt as if it were calling to me. It took me kissing Logan tonight for me to realize what it was. It was you."

"Seeing that tonight...it killed me, Elizabeth. It

made me insane with jealousy." I rolled her on her back and I propped myself up, hovering over her. My fingers crawled out to splay wide across her chest, and I pressed my hand over her heart as I stared down at the brown eyes that searched me through our misery. "Because I already knew that, Elizabeth. I already knew you belonged to me just like I belong to you." I dropped my gaze to the empty spot near her head. I tried to rein in the depth of the rage that jealousy had evoked in me. Then I sealed my eyes on hers. "You hurt me, Elizabeth. I'm not going to lie and tell you it's okay, because it's not. You are my *life*, but you have to make the decision you're going to live it with me, even when that life brings hardships we don't want to face."

Grief twisted her face, but I continued.

"And I'll never be able to express to you how sorry I am that I pushed you to let her go. It was stupid, but I thought I was protecting you and that you were just harming yourself by continuing to hang onto her all that time. I should have let you make the decision when you were ready."

Hesitant fingers fluttered along my chest. Sadness deepened the lines on her face. She fisted her hand as if she had to work up to what she wanted to say. Her voice came quiet, ragged in its admission.

"But that's the thing, Christian, I would never

have been ready to let her go. And I think you knew that. You *know* me. Know me the way no one else does, in a way no one else ever will. I blamed you for what you were never responsible for. I couldn't even look at you because you represented everything I had wanted, all of my hopes, my hopes for this little girl and for our marriage. In one day it was shattered."

She slipped her hand up my neck, cupped my jaw, her eyes burning into mine.

"I'm scared that when you and I are together, I'm so happy. It feels like every time I give myself to you, I'm hit with the worst kind of devastation. I'm scared of what you make me feel. It's so intense that sometimes it's overwhelming. But tonight, with Logan..." Frantically she gathered my hand, arched her back so she could place my palm over her heart. "No one can touch this but you. My heart, it belongs to you just like every other part of me does. All of it...all of me. I'm yours."

And I was reeling, staggered by the depth of her words. By what they meant.

"I love you, Elizabeth. Nothing can change that."

"I'm so sorry it took someone else touching me to make me realize that, to knock me back into reality. If I'd have just held on a little longer, I would have seen, Christian. I've felt a change in me, a glimmer of light when I was so lost in the darkness. I know it would have lit on you."

I brushed my lips over hers, the softest pass, an embrace.

She wound her arms around my neck and buried her face in my neck. "I'm never going to get over her."

I ragged sigh left me, because I grasped the truth of her words. They were my truth, too.

"No one expects you to get over her, Elizabeth. Neither of us will ever completely heal from it. We lost our *child*. That is something we're going to have to deal with forever. It's never going to stop hurting, but it will get better, and we have to live through it together."

We had to believe that our little girl was safe, free, that she wasn't alone or feeling any of this pain we bore for her.

Elizabeth cried, hugging me tighter.

I ran my hand through her hair, whispered at her head. "People don't always get to love like this, Elizabeth. Not the way we do. It's a gift."

I shifted so I could look down at her. "Please don't ever let it go."

the epilogues

A gentle breeze blew across the rising swell. Ocean waves tumbled in, crashing as they broke on the shore. Rays of sunlight slanted between gaps in the thin layer of clouds hanging in the late afternoon sky. My bare feet sank into the dampened sand, a feeling I had loved since I was a little girl.

Peace settled over me like the warmest embrace.

He stood on our beach just off in the distance. Locks of black hair beat at his forehead as wind gusted in. His face was still all sharp angles, his jaw strong, those lips still pouty and full.

But his eyes. They were aware, knowing and kind.

My heart stuttered as a roll of nervous energy hastened through me.

Yes, Christian Davison still managed to steal my breath. It was no different than ten years ago when he'd first walked through those cafe doors and changed the direction of my life.

I guess I should have known it then, the way he'd made me feel as if he'd knocked something loose inside of me, unleashed something I didn't know existed.

Lizzie peeked back at me. Her long black hair was all tied up in an elegant twist. It was beautiful and made her look much too old, but she insisted that she have her hair done like mine. She was almost seven, but today, as she paused and looked back at me with a meaningful smile, her mouth so soft and her blue eyes softer, I knew my little girl fully grasped what this day meant to us.

At the end of the sandy path, she veered off to the left and took her spot.

Our guests all stood and turned to face me. There were few, just two short rows of chairs situated on each side. This was the way Christian and I wanted it.

The wedding we'd missed almost a year ago was supposed to take place in a large church overflowing with all the people we knew—friends, family, and acquaintances.

Today there were only those closest to us, those who really understood what we'd gone through to make it here today.

On the left, my sister, Sarah, was surrounded by her husband and two children. Carrie, my youngest sister, smiled at me from within the mix. And my mom, she was there, her expression so kind, so gentle in the backdrop of the rough woman who had worked her entire life to take care of us. There were just a couple others, my aunt and a few cousins.

I looked to the right. Christian's aunt, a woman I had only met this week, stood there beaming, flanked by her husband who had his arm around her waist. They'd said they wouldn't have missed this, not for the world.

My attention traveled to the front row and settled on Claire. A wistful smile lifted one side of her trembling mouth. Our eyes met. Hers were glassy and red. She was already crying, twisting a handkerchief in her fingers. She mouthed, "Thank you."

Emotion expanded my chest, filled it so full, it made it difficult to breathe. But the loss of this breath was not pain as it used to be. This was joy.

It was I who owed her thanks, the one who I would be grateful to for the rest of my life for her son.

My attention was drawn to him. This beautiful man who stood there, staring at me, waiting for me, as if I were his life.

I knew I was, just as assuredly as he was mine.

Never again would I run from him.

The cellist shifted, the strings striking with the song we had chosen for this day. It wound with the wind, crashed with the waves, a soft love song that rose to a beautiful crescendo that called me home.

My steps were slow as I began to walk toward the man who had loved me through my darkest hour, my stride deliberate as my bare feet sank into the sand. The flowing gown swished around my ankles, the back brushing the ground.

Maybe my steps were slow. Maybe it was because I was relishing each one, like each represented an obstacle we'd had to climb, the trials we'd had to overcome. Maybe each one was a triumph, each a celebration.

Even though each step was measured, in reality, I was running toward him.

Running toward my forever.

Because I realized I didn't have one without Christian.

He was my all.

I stopped a foot from him. He smiled that smile, that stomach-flipping, heart-lurching, earth-shattering smile.

The one that was only for me.

Softly he tilted his head to the side, so many words spoken in his expressive eyes, his love and his devotion, his hopes and his dreams. He cupped my jaw and ran his thumb along my cheek. "You beautiful girl," he whispered into the wind.

I covered his hand with mine, pressed it closer as I closed my eyes.

And I cherished.

I cherished this man.

My eyes fluttered open and I caught Matthew's expression from where he stood behind Christian, standing up as his Best Man. What else would he be? He'd stood beside me, beside us for so long. He was our best friend, our family. His kind brown eyes swam in a soft affection, in a relief and a joy of something he'd wished for me for so many years. He'd always told me he just wanted me to be happy.

And I truly was.

Christian slipped his hand from my cheek to my neck, his palm warm against my cool skin as he dragged it down the expanse of my bare shoulder, over my elbow, all the way to my hand.

Chills flashed across my skin, his touch igniting deep within me. No longer was it unknown. This need I knew well. It was something only found in him, a safety and a charge of desire.

He knotted our fingers together as we turned to

face the minister who stood in front of the simple floral arbor.

Natalie stepped forward, kissed my cheek as she took my bouquet. My Matron of Honor stepped back behind Lizzie. Her smile was wide, as if she were fighting a grin, uncontained delight rising in her as she looked at Christian and me, as we began a new leg of the journey we'd started so many years ago.

And with my family surrounding me, the people who'd seen me through so much, I promised my life to Christian.

Our vows were simple.

I will stand by you forever.

We already knew what that meant, that there would be difficulties we would face, that there would be sorrow. But there would also be joy.

And I was going to live every day of those with Christian.

The minister pronounced us husband and wife. Christian turned to me, and for a few moments, we just stood there looking at each other. This beautiful man who had touched me, who'd changed me and shaped the person I had become.

His hold was gentle as he reached out and took my face between his hands, his fingers splayed wide as he tilted my face up to meet his penetrating gaze.

The wind gusted around us, the smell of the

ocean riding on the cool, spring breeze. Errant strands of my hair blew all around us, whipping at our skin and stirring up our spirits.

Blue eyes blazed as they looked down on me. For a flash, his hold tightened, and in it, he made another promise.

I will never let you go.

Then his mouth descended on mine, his hands on my face and his grip on my soul. This kiss was slow, maddening, fire and ice, always too much and never enough. My fingers found their way into the jacket of his tux as he bent me back. Passion ripped through us before we tripped into this consuming joy. And then he was grinning at my mouth, and I was laughing and crying as I wrapped my arms around his head. He pulled me off my feet and into his arms, spinning me around.

"I love you, Elizabeth Davison."

I leaned back so I could see his face. "I love you, Christian. Forever."

Lizzie giggled, rushed to our side as Christian set me back on my feet. He hoisted her up in his arms. Today, she didn't seem to complain, but just grinned as she wrapped herself around his neck, Christian's grip firm around my waist.

I stood there swaying in the arms of my little family. Cheers rose up from the small gathering, those who were there because they loved us, because they wished the best for our lives, as they showered us with their blessings, supported our hopes and these undying dreams.

And I was happy. Intensely. Wholly.

Giggles rolled up my throat as I buried my fingers in Christian's hair. I lifted my face to the mirrored ceiling, his mouth at my neck. He had me pressed up against the elevator wall as it lifted and sped toward the top floor of the hotel.

"Mmm…you smell so good." A brush of his mouth, a nip of his teeth.

I moaned as I tightened my hold.

A groan rumbled in his chest, and he kissed along my collarbone.

The elevator dinged and the doors parted. Christian's head shot up, just as fast as the smirk shot to his face. He grabbed my hand, hauling me behind him as he fumbled for the keycard, as if he couldn't make it to our room fast enough.

He suddenly swung me around in front of him and whisked me into his arms. I yelped before I snuggled into the perfection of his hold, winding my arms around his neck.

He maneuvered so he could slide the keycard into the slot, and then kicked the door open wide.

"Aren't you supposed to carry me over the threshold of our house, not our hotel room?" I flashed a teasing grin up at him, my mouth curved with the force of this love.

He angled to the side so we could fit through the door. Amusement sparked in his eyes, glinted with his joy. "Well, I'd be happy to do that, too. But tonight, I'm carrying my wife through this door, and once I get her behind it, I'm going to make love to her again and again. You don't have a problem with that, do you, Mrs. Davison?"

I laughed a little more, not able to comprehend this bliss, the way I felt, a buzz of energy burning below my skin as Christian carried me into the suite at the highest point of Downtown San Diego.

He brought us into the expansive suite. Candles glowed all around the living area, flickering as they jumped and twinkled against the floor-to-ceiling windows facing the bay. Black waters rippled and danced in the moonlight that hung low in the darkened sky.

"Who did this?" I whispered.

"I might have had a little help from your sisters and Natalie. That's why they left the reception a little early."

I bit my lip to bite back my awe, turned my red face into the collar of his white button-up and breathed in this magnificent man. Hours ago, he'd rid himself of the stuffy jacket and pulled off his tie.

I still couldn't decide if I liked him better in a tux or in his low-slung jeans.

His dress shoes echoed on the marble floor as he crossed the living area into the bedroom. Here, too, candles sat on every surface. Flames flickered and danced, casting shadows across the large bed covered in plush, white linens, the bedding turned down and waiting for us, and a mass of floral bouquets filled the space.

In the background, our song played.

"I didn't need all of this," I whispered into the calm of the room.

"No, but I can give it to you, so why would I not?" His expression shifted, his jaw held taut. The playfulness that had followed us all the way from our reception party, into the limo, and here to our suite faded away. In its place was a distinct intensity, his expression severe. Lines deepened on his brow. A dense weight filled the room, and, in the short flickers of the flames, I watched the emotion gather on his face.

Slowly he lowered me to my feet.

A thick knot formed in my throat when Christian stepped back, his brazen gaze caressing my body.

The hair piled high on my head was beginning to fall apart with the play of this evening, the dancing and the kisses and the hands that Christian couldn't seem to keep out of the intricate twist. Pieces hung loose, brushing down over my bare shoulders and tumbling to the top of my strapless gown.

It was the same dress that had hung in a garment bag in the back of my closet for many months, the one I'd been so eager to stand before Christian in as I promised him my life. It had to be altered, the dress originally made to accommodate my swollen belly, but this dress had always been for him.

I felt beautiful wearing it in front of him now.

He trailed his fingertips down my jaw, let them linger at the hollow of my neck. "You are the most exquisite woman, Elizabeth. No one compares to you. Not a single soul."

I trembled at his touch, shook with his words.

How was it possible he still made me feel this way?

He took me by the shoulders and guided me to turn. His breath washed against the back of my neck.

The fine hairs at my nape lifted, and chills sped down my spine.

Adept fingers worked on the tiny pearl button at the top of the gown's zipper. Goosebumps flashed across my flesh as Christian freed it and began to drag the zipper down, my skin slowly exposed.

The gown pooled in a heap at my feet.

"Beautiful," he whispered.

I wore a white bustier that dropped low in the back, the satin-lined bodice pressing my breasts together in the lift, matching panties that were all satin and lace, and a pair of white heels I'd slipped on when we left the beach.

For a moment, we just stood there, Christian's presence burning into me from behind.

Finally, he touched me, his palms gliding down my hips to my thighs, before he trailed them back up, applying pressure as he turned me around. His mouth curved in gentle affection when he took my hand and helped me step from the mound of fabric bunched on the floor.

Christian took a step back, let his eyes wander as he contemplated every inch of me.

A blush blossomed across my chest and spread all the way to my cheeks. The man had seen me at my worst and seen me at my best, and he'd made love to me countless times. Still, his gaze slipped over me in a slow appreciation, as if he were undressing me for the very first time.

A strip of bare skin was exposed between the bodice and my panties, and Christian's attention dropped to it. He reached out, his right thumb making a tender pass over the tattoo that rested on the front of my left hip.

The tiny black bird had spread her wings, her spirit free.

My Lillie.

Christian had one that matched.

We'd gone together, another step that felt as if

we were slowly healing. I'd come to realize that I was scared that moving on meant I had to let her go. Now I knew that wasn't true. Even though we hadn't been allowed to keep her here, she would forever live in our hearts.

Our forever.

She would always hold a piece of that.

I would always feel the loss of Lillie. Her memory would always hurt, but I'd learned to find joy in her, in the love that Christian and I shared for her, in the unending hope that I realized we needed to carry on in her name.

Christian cupped my face between his hands, a storm of intensity brewing in his eyes. "I love you, Elizabeth. More than you will ever know. You have absolutely made me the happiest man alive."

I smoothed my fingertips against the sharp angles of his jaw, let them flutter up to trace the curve of his lips. "But I do know, Christian. Because there is no way to love you more than I love you now. No greater joy than this."

His hands slid down my neck and over the cap of my shoulders. He leaned to reach behind me, ticking off the little clasps that held together the lingerie.

A rush of cool splashed against my skin, and my nipples pebbled as they met with the air. Christian dipped his head, took over my mouth, his kiss strong and slow as he circled my breasts with the pad of his thumbs.

A tiny moan slipped up my throat. Christian devoured it as he intensified his kiss, stroked my tongue with his.

I nipped at his bottom lip as I sought out the button on his waistband, worked it free, rushed through the buttons on his shirt. My palms came flat to his chest, and I pushed his shirt free from his shoulders.

Kicking off his shoes and socks, Christian twisted out of the shirt. I edged down his pants, taking his underwear with them.

My eyes wandered and traced, adoring this beautiful man that I loved with every ounce of my life.

He scooped me up and placed me in the center of the bed, his muscles rippling as he crawled up to me. He grasped me by the knees, slowly pressing them apart as he ran his palms up the inside of my thighs.

A trail of fire burned in his wake and throbbed between my legs.

He twisted his fingers in the edges of my panties and dragged them down, leaning in to brush his lips in a tortuous path behind them.

"Christian, please."

The man was always making me beg.

A soft chuckle rolled from him as he moved to hover over me, dipped down to kiss me, long and hard. He hummed, the sound a vibration from his mouth that shot straight through me. He let his fingers wander between my thighs, brushed his knuckles across the sensitive skin.

I moaned.

"Look at you," he whispered as he settled between my legs. His erection slipped against my folds. One hand cupped my jaw, and he tilted my chin up to him. "My wife."

Then he took me whole, body and soul. All of me. Always.

Our bodies bonded, we moved slowly. My fingers were woven in the promise of his, and he kept them nested between our chests. We were nose-to-nose, breath-to-breath.

Christian stared down at me as he made love to me for the first time as my husband, the man I was giving all of my days.

Our lives had taken us in so many directions. We'd been granted so much joy and burdened with so much sorrow. We'd been forced down roads we didn't want to take, blinded by the unforeseen, taken detours that had led us to the unexpected.

My eyes were locked on the one who waited at the end of my every path. My destiny. The one I could never escape.

"I love you, Christian," I whispered, a promise, an oath.

Christian nuzzled me beneath my ear, then

tipped his mouth to whisper in it. "We made it, Elizabeth."

And Christian loved me, the way only he could.

And I knew it. Knew he would be my forever.

ONE YEAR LATER
CHRISTIAN

I stood at the large window, peering out into the near dark.

When the night had grown deep, I'd climbed from bed where I'd lain for hours, unable to sleep. I'd crept across the bedroom, drawn to the peaceful scene painted outside.

The quarter moon hung low in the sky. It glinted across the murky waters of the raging sea. Tree branches beat at the walls, a squall of heavy wind lashing at the earth. In the distance, waves rushed up the shore and crashed on the beach.

I could stand here for hours. Just listening, lost in my thoughts.

Five months ago, we'd finally found the perfect house. It was a beautiful structure, five bedrooms, a kitchen Elizabeth would be happy to live in, and a sweeping backyard.

Yeah. It backed up to our beach.

Lizzie spent entire days out playing on the lawn, pumping her legs furiously on her swing, walking hand in hand with her mother, barefoot in the sand.

As much as we loved it here, Elizabeth and I knew the walls themselves meant nothing. It was what filled them that counted, the laughter that echoed from them, the happiness they contained.

Joy reigned here.

That didn't mean there were no bad days. There were still times when I found Elizabeth on her knees in the huge walk-in closet adjoining our bedroom. Lillie's blanket would be balled in her arms. She'd rock it as if she were rocking the child she never truly had the chance to. She'd cry and she'd whisper incoherent words, she'd love and she'd adore. Then she'd dry her eyes and climb to her feet, tucking those precious tokens away until she felt compelled to be immersed in them again. She'd never had the strength to leave them out, to put any of it on display, but instead hid it away as her own buried treasure.

I'd be waiting for her, leaning up against the doorframe. Elizabeth would cast me a mournful smile as I pulled her into my arms, and she'd mumble into my shirt how much she missed her.

And we were okay with that, welcomed those days because, even though they hurt, they belonged to Lillie.

Another wave crashed, and the ocean stirred.

Behind me, our bed creaked, a soft rustle of

sheets. I looked over my shoulder.

Elizabeth sat up on the side of the bed, arching as she pressed her hands to her lower back. Her long hair fell in waves as she lifted her chin, brushed along the bed as she stretched her neck.

My breath caught.

Beauty. There was no other way to describe it.

She'd always reminded me of honey, the golden glow of her skin, the sweetness of her mouth, the warmth in her eyes.

I started toward her, whispering, "What are you doing awake, baby? You need to rest."

She blinked at me through the shadows of the darkened room. She almost pouted. "Too uncomfortable."

She blew a strained breath between pursed lips.

I crouched down between her knees. My fingers crawled up the top of her legs and around to her back where I massaged deeply into her hips where she always seemed to be sore.

She whimpered out a subdued moan. "That feels so good."

"I wish I could do more."

"Just keep doing what you're doing and I'm a happy girl."

Her fitted tank top had ridden up, bunched just below her swollen breasts. The huge protrusion ballooned out between us, her belly button stretched thin.

Elizabeth was five days passed her due date.

A smile tugged at the corner of my mouth.

Apparently my son was stubborn.

Three months after our wedding, we found out Elizabeth was pregnant again. News of this pregnancy hadn't been met with the thrill of the last, with the wild expectation for what was to be. Instead it'd been met with trembling hands and trepidation.

But we'd realized this life was worth the chance, that we had to breathe and live and love, and we couldn't allow fear to hold us back.

It didn't mean there weren't the nagging worries, the panic that would tighten Elizabeth's eyes if she thought it'd been too long since she last felt him move.

For our peace of mind, Dr. Montieth had recommended that we get a home heart monitor. She'd taught us how to use it, what to look for and what to be concerned of, the quickened whirl of his heartbeat a promise that he was okay.

Elizabeth looked down as she ran her hand over her stomach, bit her lip as she glanced up at me under the hedge of hair that had fallen in her face.

I reached up and brushed it back.

She cradled him between her hands. "I wish he would come," she whispered. A smile trembled at her mouth. "I can't wait to meet him."

I slipped my hands around her sides and to her

front, covered Elizabeth's hold in mine as we swam in our anticipation. "I've never been more ready for anything, Elizabeth."

She smiled a little before a yawn overtook her. She chuckled as she tried to conceal it behind her hand.

I nudged her chin with the hook of my index finger. "You need to get some rest. I have a feeling you're not going to get much of it really soon."

She giggled in the cutest way. "Yeah, I guess he can't hide out in here forever."

I crawled in bed with her, pulled the covers over us as I nestled her back against my chest. She curled into me, her tender hand covering mine where I rested it on the distended wall of her belly.

Contentment thrummed between us.

Her breaths evened out like a soothing balm, and she quickly drew me into sleep.

A thrill of energy rose up in the room, a cheer of encouragement. "You're almost there, Elizabeth. Give me one more big push," Dr. Montieth coaxed.

Sweat drenched Elizabeth's forehead, soaked her hair. She clenched my hand as she bore down and cried out.

For a moment, there was silence as our son slipped into Dr. Montieth's hands. Time seemed to stop as I watched the frantic movements that had slowed in my mind. The doctor held him in a blue blanket, one hand at the back of his neck as she almost tipped him upside down, the other suctioning out his mouth and nose.

Blood stained him, covered him whole, this little boy that already held my heart.

My vision blurred.

Then he cried.

These shrill, shocked cries that welcomed him into this world.

Another blanket was tossed on Elizabeth's belly, and they set him on his side, the two nurses roughing it over his tiny body.

And he was crying and crying. The precious sound rattled through the room as his little arms and legs flailed.

Shaking uncontrollably, Elizabeth reached for him, palmed his head with an unsteady hand. He reacted, tilting against her touch as if seeking her out, a stutter in his cries as his mouth twisted at the side because the child already knew her.

And she wept, tears of relief and tears of joy, a torrent of emotion spilling from this amazing woman. From the woman who held my dreams, the one who held my future.

I rushed to smooth her hair back that was drenched in sweat, dropped my forehead to hers, lost myself in the warmth of her brown eyes. "You did it," flooded as a desperate whisper as I kissed her mouth, as I kissed the woman I loved with all my life, "You beautiful girl. You did it."

I stood at the window, peering out into the night, rocking in a slow sway. Waves rushed in, crashed on the shore. A contented sigh flowed from me as I rocked from side to side.

Myles squirmed in the safety of my hold, cradled in my arm. It was a writhe, the little guy worming around with a restless roll, extending his head back.

I couldn't hold in my smile.

I'd been right.

My son was stubborn. He knew exactly what he wanted and when he wanted it.

Stretching his free leg, he flexed his foot, digging his toes into my skin. Tight against the side of his face, he clenched and unclenched one tiny fist. He jerked his open mouth toward my chest, his tongue jutting out between his lips as if he were searching, hunting.

But of course he was.

He wanted his mother.

Jerking the other direction, he fought with his fist, trying to stuff it into his mouth. He was making all these little noises, rattled sounds that were not quite a cry.

"Shh…" I rocked him a little, the softest

bounce. "Let's let mommy sleep just a little longer. Do you think you could do that? It's not quite time for you to eat yet."

At the sound of my muted voice, he looked up at me with his wide, storm-blue eyes.

Love consumed me, filled every crevice of my being as I looked down at his perfect face.

My son.

Elizabeth insisted those dark blue eyes would turn the color of mine. She said Lizzie's had been so much the same. I wasn't sold on it yet. His hair was light, a thin layer that didn't even cover the cap of his head, like maybe he was going to take after his mother, this beautiful child that had completed our home.

He fussed a little more, and I began to pace the floor, hoping to give Elizabeth a few more minutes sleep.

I lifted him to nuzzle his cheek. "Why don't we go check on your big sister?" I murmured at the softness of his skin.

I chuckled low when his mouth bobbed at my cheek, rooting, seeking, exploring. Tiny fingernails scratched at my face, their dig like an embrace that went straight to my heart. I kissed the tips of his fingers as they tugged at my lips.

I crept from mine and Elizabeth's room, through the living space, to the other end of the house. Lizzie's door sat partially open, the nightlight that glowed from within illuminating her precious face in subdued light.

She was fast asleep, lost in her dreams, that sweet face relaxed as she rested on her pillow, her hair billowing out behind her.

I nudged the door farther open, walked to her side, and brushed my fingers through my daughter's silky black hair.

This little girl who had once stopped me in my tracks with a penetrating gaze and a tiny smile that had undone something in me. The one who had covered me in awareness, the one who'd sent love rushing in.

This child, the one who had been mine and Elizabeth's breaking point, the one who had also been our start. The catalyst with her knowing eyes and tender heart.

She was the one who had changed the selfish person I was.

I'd never stop wishing I could go back and change it. Getting to experience this with Myles…I'd never really known just how much I'd missed. And I *missed* it. Wished for it. That I could hold Lizzie as a baby.

In the depths of sleep, she released a soft sigh, an emotion that was palpable as it wound with my heart, like maybe this intuitive child understood.

All I had was today, and I chose to love her with every second, with every breath.

Leaning down, I swept a small kiss across Lizzie's cheek.

She was the most amazing big sister, too, the way I'd always imagined she'd be. She couldn't wait for Myles to get a little older, to hear the first of his laughter, to watch his first smile grace his face. She couldn't wait for him to play.

I hugged my six-week-old son a little closer to me, willing time to slow. I'd learned to cherish each day, and I wished none of them away.

He fussed, and a tiny cry gurgled from his trembling mouth, his toothless gums exposed.

My chest tightened, affection pressed.

Was it strange I thought it the cutest thing?

I whispered to Lizzie, "Goodnight, princess," then kissed her again before I lifted Myles to the center of my chest. He curled his legs up under him, tucked into a tiny ball. I patted his back as I walked back through the house, pressed my lips to the crown of his head.

I entered back into the muted light and looked down to where my wife lay. Awake, she was on her side, facing me. A sleepy smile spread along her gorgeous mouth.

"I thought I heard him crying. Is he hungry?"

I nodded with a smirk, my palm a caress at the back of his head. "Apparently this little guy likes you as much as I do."

Her smile transformed as a blush crawled across

her face, the sweet innocence that had stolen my heart hinting at her cheeks. "He does, huh? Well, I kind of like him, too."

With our son in my arms, I placed a knee on the mattress and climbed to the bed. I passed Myles to her, and she welcomed him into her arms.

Light filled her face. Intense, radiant light. It shined with love. With joy.

Still lying on her side, she nestled him against her, lifted her arm over her head as she bunched up her shirt so Myles could find her breast.

He curled back into that tiny ball, his fingers fisted in her shirt. He grunted, jerked his head and mouth as he latched on.

Elizabeth caressed the back of her hand over his round cheek, looked down at the child who had taught us so many things—that it was okay to hope again, to love without fear, even when it might cost us all, to show it every day.

I settled down beside them, our son cocooned between us.

She glanced up at me, her brown eyes steeped in emotion. "I didn't think I'd ever love this much again."

I reached across the short space, held her face in the cup of my hand, and realized I'd never felt closer to her than I did now.

Her gaze locked with mine, this woman who loved me with everything and trusted me with all.

My mind rushed through the years of our lives, what my hopes for the future held.

The footsteps that would clamor over these wooden floors, the laughter and the play, the days that would pass as we watched our children grow. I could picture Myles stumbling across the lawn on unsure feet, the biggest grin on his face, Lizzie at his side, encouraging him to take one more step.

The way it would sound when he called me *Daddy*.

The way my little girl would slowly turn into a woman, how it terrified me yet made me insane with pride at the same time.

How my children would learn. All their missteps and triumphs, failures and successes.

How one day they would find a love of their own.

How Elizabeth and I would be allowed to grow old together.

That we'd love until we'd been given no more days, and then, somehow, I'd find her again.

This woman, the one who'd stolen my breath with a passing glance.

This woman, the one who'd changed every piece of me.

I clutched her face as I kissed her.

This woman.

My forever.

the end

I invite you to sign up for mobile updates to receive short, but sweet updates on all my latest releases.
Text "aljackson" to 33222
(US Only)
or
Sign up for my newsletter
http://smarturl.it./NewsFromALJackson

Watch for my upcoming series, *Confessions of the Heart*, coming Fall 2018!

Want to know when it's live?
Sign up here: http://smarturl.it/liveonamzn

More From A.L. Jackson

ABOUT THE AUTHOR

A.L. Jackson is the New York Times & USA Today Bestselling author of contemporary romance. She writes emotional, sexy, heart-filled stories about boys who usually like to be a little bit bad.

Her bestselling series include THE REGRET SERIES, CLOSER TO YOU, BLEEDING STARS, as well as the newest FIGHT FOR ME novels.

Watch for her new series, CONFESSIONS OF THE HEART, coming Fall 2018

If she's not writing, you can find her hanging out by the pool with her family, sipping cocktails with her friends, or of course with her nose buried in a book.

Be sure not to miss new releases and sales from A.L. Jackson - Sign up to receive her newsletter http://smarturl.it/NewsFromALJackson or text "aljackson" to 33222 to receive short but sweet updates on all the important news.

Connect with A.L. Jackson online:

Page **http://smarturl.it/ALJacksonPage**
Newsletter **http://smarturl.it/NewsFromALJackson**
Angels **http://smarturl.it/AmysAngelsRock**
Amazon **http://smarturl.it/ALJacksonAmzn**
Book Bub **http://smarturl.it/ALJacksonBookbub**
Text "aljackson" to 33222 to receive short but sweet updates on all the important news.